Of Dreams and Assassins

CARAF Books

Caribbean and African Literature
Translated from French

Carrol F. Coates, Editor

Clarisse Zimra, J. Michael Dash, John Conteh-Morgan,
and Elisabeth Mudimbe-Boyi, Advisory Editors

Of Dreams and Assassins

Malika Mokeddem

Translated and with an Introduction by
K. Melissa Marcus

University Press of Virginia

CHARLOTTESVILLE AND LONDON

Publication of this translation was assisted by a grant
from the French Ministry of Culture

Originally published in French as *Des rêves et des assassins*
© Editions Grasset & Fasquelle, 1995

THE UNIVERSITY PRESS OF VIRGINIA

♾ The paper used in this publication meets the minimum
requirements of the American National Standard for
Information Sciences—Permanence of Paper for Printed
Library Materials, ANSI Z39.48-1984.

Library of Congress Cataloging-in-Publication Data
Mokeddem, Malika.
 [Des rêves et des assassins. English]
 Of dreams and assassins / Malika Mokeddem ; translated and with an
introduction by K. Melissa Marcus.
  p. cm. — (CARAF books) (Caribbean and African literature
translated from French)
  ISBN 0-8139-1933-9 (cloth). — ISBN 0-8139-1994-0 (pbk. : alk. paper)
  I. Marcus, K. Melissa, 1956– . II. Title. III. Series.
IV. Series: Caribbean and African literature translated from French.
PQ3989.2.M55D4713 2000
843—dc21   99-43291
                                                              CIP

Contents

Acknowledgments   vii

Introduction   ix

Bibliography   xxx

Emptiness and Excess   5

The Unexpected and the Worst   16

Sinful Love   27

False Loves   35

When Knowledge Is the First Exile   47

Montpellier   61

Slim the Glider   72

Dreams of Two Souths   86

Words Like Sequins   96

Toward Other White Lands   110

Glossary   121

Acknowledgments

Des rêves et des assassins is the second of Mokeddem's four novels to appear in English. I would like to express my warm thanks to several people. I am very grateful to Maguy Albet for having introduced me personally to Malika Mokeddem; to Marie-Hélène d'Ovidio of Editions Grasset for her help, constant interest in the translation of Mokeddem's work, hospitality, and kindness in Paris; to my dear friend, colleague, and fellow translator Marilya Veteto-Conrad; and to my mother, Arlen Bishop, for her repeated and careful proofreading of my work. I sincerely thank my editor Carrol Coates for his support of this project and his encouragement, patience, and professionalism. Louella Holter's editorial prowess helped me immensely. I am grateful to Rachid Aadnani for providing the transliterations of Arabic words. Finally, I would like to warmly thank the author herself, Malika Mokeddem, for her hospitality in France, her help in answering my many questions, and above all, her exceedingly courageous literary, political, and personal stance.

An earlier version of my translation of the chapter "Emptiness and Excess" was published in *Callaloo* 20, no. 1 (winter 1997): 20–27. © Charles H. Rowell. Reprinted by permission of the Johns Hopkins University Press.

Introduction

In a 1994 interview Malika Mokeddem stated, "All my life I have waged a battle to be who I want to be in the face of a society that wanted to crush women. I dedicated myself to my studies, to the battle for women's rights, but I was suffocating. I had to leave. That is my failure. I write in order to raise my voice from southern France, a voice other than that put forth by the [Muslim] fanatics, and to rid myself of this feeling of failure. I am from both coasts, a woman flayed alive, but also an angry woman."[1]

Of Dreams and Assassins, Malika Mokeddem's fourth novel, set in contemporary Algeria, is a novel about struggle and unfulfilled dreams—the struggle of one woman, Kenza, and through her, the struggle of many Algerian women. Kenza struggles and dreams of doing many things in her native country: experiencing love and openly expressing it, leading the life of an independent and successful career woman, acting of her own volition, speaking freely, smoking in public, going to a bar. At the core of this novel is a young woman's search for freedom in a repressive society, dominated by the imperatives of Islamic fundamentalism and restrictive traditions, and her search for a mother she never knew—a search that will lead to the forging of her own identity and her finding the strength to make fundamental changes in her life.

Much of Mokeddem's writing derives directly from her own life experiences, although none of her novels is strictly autobiographical. It is thus important to understand her childhood, her youth, and the environment in which she grew up to fully appreciate the context in which she writes.

Born in Kenadsa, Algeria, a small mining town on the edge of the desert, Malika Mokeddem spent her childhood in a *qsar*, a traditional village with earthen structures. She was the oldest of thirteen children, three of whom died very young, and the daughter of

Introduction

illiterate nomads who had settled down only recently. Her first novel, *The Men Who Walk*, although not an autobiography, retraces her life as a child and adolescent through the heroine, Leïla, and tells the story of how, over several generations, her family became sedentary. (She uses her family members' real first names.) We also see pieces of Algerian history: the awakening of the resistance against colonialism several years before the outbreak of war, the war for independence from France (1954–62), and the gaining of independence itself.

Mokeddem grew up listening to the stories of her Bedouin paternal grandmother, Zohra, who was a nomad most of her life, becoming sedentary only at an advanced age. Mokeddem was born at the beginning of her father's sedentary life, and her mother, from Morocco, was a city cousin from another branch of the family, but Mokeddem was constantly cradled in the nomad culture of her grandmother. Mokeddem describes her grandmother as very much out of place, an "exile" in sedentary life: "She had the speech of a person in exile. She had been torn from that life, and for her, too, there remained only words to continue to make her past stay alive."[2]

Indeed, Mokeddem attributes her lifelong interest in words to her grandmother's prowess as a storyteller: "It is for this reason that the oral tradition is something of great importance to me, because I think . . . that before books, my first sensitivity to words came through my grandmother."[3] (The importance of the oral mode is clear in Mokeddem's third novel, *The Forbidden Woman*, in which the women of the village speak in a veritable Greek chorus as a means of expressing long-repressed feelings and anger.) Mokeddem's grandmother allowed her to dream through her stories. She opened the beauty and wonders of the desert to her, despite its oppressive summer heat, which kept the girl mostly indoors for months at a time. Mokeddem summons up this desert world in the first chapter of *Of Dreams and Assassins,* an evocation based largely on her own experiences. The desert's immensity is present as a liberating force in all of her novels, both literally and symbolically, because of its lack of borders. Yet it is also in the desert that Mokeddem felt, and her heroines feel, more enclosed, because of the societal and cultural constraints they experience there. This contradiction becomes a leitmotiv in her work.

Although raised in a tolerant strain of Islam, Mokeddem began her battles early against the weight of tradition and custom. As the

Introduction

oldest girl, she was expected to carry out many household chores, an imperative against which she rebelled at a young age. But partly through the influence of her grandmother, she became the only girl in her family and in her village to attend secondary school in the neighboring town of Béchar, and once there, she was the only girl in a class of forty-five students. The story of why Mokeddem was put in school became a truth-based legend, as she recounts: "Before us, there had been an ancestor . . . who had been put into a *medersa*, thinking that he was going to become a great master of the Koran, and he had become a poet, and that wasn't at all approved of. . . . He had pretty much been banished from his tribe because of writing, and my grandmother, . . . the destiny of this man had so much eaten at her that she had made of it a myth. She had taken her revenge and had gone as far as to put me in school."[4]

Mokeddem began school in 1955, one year after the start of Algeria's war of independence from France. She thus also attributes her schooling to the beginning of an awakening of political consciousness. In school she was one of a tiny handful of girls, for at that time, families tended to put only their boys in school. Also, the bourgeoisie educated its children, but the peasants and the nomads did not. Furthermore, estimates Mokeddem, at the time of Algeria's independence, only 10 percent of Algeria's children were in school.[5] Considering the circumstances, it was miraculous that Malika was put in school, and schooling became her path to freedom from the societal and familial traditions under which she so chafed. To this day, she recognizes how much she owes to the school and to her teachers who made it clear that her way to a different world would be achieved through education: "The teacher said to me: 'Your battle is to succeed in your studies, and that's how things will get better, that's how we'll succeed in changing the world.'"[6]

After the tales of her grandmother, which opened up the nomadic world to her, then, came books, which nourished her desire to escape and placed in her the seeds of her exile. In 1962 (the year of Algeria's independence), at the age of twelve, Mokeddem went to *collège* (secondary school), and for several years, until she completed her baccalaureate, she remained the only girl in her class.

Mokeddem saw the women around her as being closed in like a many-layered Russian doll. They were closed inside of the house and village by both custom and necessity—cloistered off from the world and from the desert heat. Although school provided for her an escape, she nevertheless developed a problem of identity, not knowing to which world she belonged—that of her family or that of her school, which exposed her even more to French and western European cultures. The resulting feelings of alienation are a continual theme in her writing, in particular in *The Forbidden Woman* and *Of Dreams and Assassins,* both of which feature female heroines endlessly caught in the struggle to negotiate two cultures, Algerian and French, with all of the attendant contradictions and differences.

Mokeddem spent her summers home from boarding school inside the house, sheltered from the ferocious heat of the Saharan desert. As her increased knowledge and learning alienated her from her surroundings—the first of many exiles—she furthered that distance by reading late into the night and sleeping half the day. She discovered a multitude of different worlds by immersing herself in the literary classics of Sartre, Beauvoir, Faulkner, and Dostoyevsky, among others. With wry amusement, Mokeddem quotes her mother: "There was always a book between me and my daughter."[7] She experienced not merely a distancing from her origins but indeed the first of several states of an exile that would culminate in her departure from Algeria.

Mokeddem also broke with tradition by refusing an arranged marriage. When an elderly uncle arranged the visit of a potential suitor's mother, Mokeddem climbed out of the window and hid for the day. "I saw my mother, I saw the women closed up inside their houses and subjugated. I did not want to become one of them. I did not want to grow up. I dreamed of going into the desert to die, to be devoured by jackals. I became anorexic."[8] This was only one of several attempts to arrange her marriage, and each time she resisted like a "Fury," as she referred to herself. Such tenacity, anger, and resistance and a constant combative stance are elements that also characterize her heroines.

Mokeddem left the desert after finishing her baccalaureate, and she began her medical studies in Oran, where she began to develop a higher political consciousness. She became disillusioned by the lack of protest on the part of the university students and felt more and more isolated and suffocated. Feeling there was no place for women of her ilk in her society, in 1977 she decided to leave. At that point it was not a decision to leave definitively; however, Mokeddem now lives permanently in France. She completed her medical studies in Montpellier, specializing in nephrology, and es-

Introduction

tablished a practice in the same city. Later, she left her specialization and opened a general practitioner's office, serving especially the needs of women, in the Maghrebian neighborhood of Montpellier. It is during this time, in the mid-1980s that she began to write.

Mokeddem explains that when she first began writing, she was the only one to believe that anything might come of her desire to write—only she believed she might really become a writer. For she was intending to put aside, in part, a medical profession in which she had had great success, and her friends warned her against throwing away a well-established career. Her need to write, she says, was based on her need to "return" to her past in Algeria. Writing helped calm her conflicted feelings about her country and made her feel less tormented. She says she continues to carry pain and guilt about having left Algeria.[9]

Mokeddem divides her time between writing and her medical practice. However, she was forced to leave her general practitioner's office after receiving death threats in February 1995, presumably from Islamic extremists in France, although the specific group was never identified. (The death threats were in response to her general outspokenness about the Islamic extremists and particularly to the critical stance she took in her third novel, *The Forbidden Woman*. She spent all of 1995 under police surveillance.) She went on to work outside of Montpellier for several days at a time in a dialysis clinic. Her work as a nephrologist is quite lucrative, allowing her to work only part-time and thus to continue to write on her days off. She claims: "I practice medicine on the one hand, and in a certain sense I have my own medicine, which is writing."[10] She also appreciates the balance she has achieved between writing and practicing medicine, a balance she claims renders her writing a pleasure not subjected to the demands of the literary world. Medicine removes her from the solitude of writing, and writing brings her back to herself.

Although frightened at the time by the death threats, Mokeddem maintains that she will never be silenced and that she will continue writing even if threatened again. In this, she is a highly political and politicized writer, seeing her writing as a mission in addition to its being a personal daily need. She and many others look to Tajar Djaout, a writer and journalist assassinated by Islamist extremists in 1993, who stressed the critical importance of continuing

Introduction

to write and to be creative in one's artistic endeavors no matter what the consequences. Mokeddem's reaction to the extremists is: "*They* have machine guns, *we* have words. That's it."[11]

It is through words, then, that Mokeddem expresses the voice of Algerian women. The anger evident in *Of Dreams and Assassins* is the anger of many. The novel is solidly anchored in current events: Mokeddem has deftly woven the complex social and political context of Algeria's postindependence years into a novel that is both personal and an expression of solidarity with her people (a solidarity mostly with women but also with men, as both are victims of Algeria's recent upheavals).

The country has seen rampant change in the second half of the twentieth century. After the Algerian Revolution, socialism, Arabization, and secularism were among the guiding principles with which Muslim Algeria was to be rebuilt. "The Algerian nationalists adopted as their official slogan 'to catch up on the accumulated delay caused during 130 years of colonial domination.' In a context marked by the emergence of Third World countries onto the international political scene and because of the development of Arab nationalism by the strong personality of Egypt's Nasser, Algeria opted resolutely for a socialist path of development."[12] The result was a glaring contrast, or even contradiction, between an officially socialist regime supportive of liberation movements around the globe and a society living according to the imperatives of the Muslim religion. The single ruling party, the Front de Libération Nationale (National Liberation Front), or FLN, allowed the patriarchal and Arab-Muslim traditions already in place to rule the private spheres of Algerian life.

Algerian women from all classes had participated fully in the war of independence. They took part in the underground as messengers, bomb and weapon carriers, and nurses. They hid, fed, and protected resistance fighters. They were arrested, often tortured, and held in prison camps, just like the men. It was therefore assumed by the women themselves and by outside observers on the international scene that Algeria's independence would be accompanied by the liberation of women and their recognition as equals. One of the most famous theorists of the colonial condition, Franz Fanon, argued essentially that women's participation in the war would suffice to radically change attitudes and mentalities and therefore the status of women.[13]

Introduction

Led by Ahmed Ben Bella, the new socialist society formed in 1962 after Algeria's victory promised women equal and full participation in Algerian society, such as had not previously been the case. But as Mokeddem explains, this was not to be so: "The women lost everything. . . . At the time of Algeria's independence, not a single woman, even among the great fighters in the war, had any parcel of power, even though there were intellectuals, someone like Franz Fanon, for example, who said that Algerian women had acquired through their use of weapons the right to equality between the sexes."[14]

However, theorists like Fanon did not predict the importance of Islam, among other factors, in keeping women in their subordinate role. For in reconstructing the identity of Algeria after 130 years of often brutal colonial rule under France, Islam became a mobilizing and unifying ideology, a principle of resistance against the colonial ideology. Religious practices were thus valued again, and women, seen as the upholders of Islamic ideology, were not allowed to move into the public sphere and assume significant positions of power. They were to be the guarantors of the stability of family, religion, and tradition. The precolonial time was seen almost as a "golden age," when Algeria's original societal structures were still in place.[15] Religious observance and nationalism went hand in hand, and many nationalists who had little by little dropped their religious observances were now forced by societal pressure to observe the first Ramadan after independence.

The twenty-year influence of the Islamic fundamentalists led to the writing of one of the most reactionary and retrograde family codes in North Africa. This code, passed in 1984, institutionalized the unequal status of Algerian women in many areas, including matters of personal autonomy, divorce, property ownership, polygamy, and work outside of the home. It codified practices already in effect in the daily treatment of women. Men were empowered legally over women in most areas. Women's groups, whose members included former revolutionaries, rallied against the code's passage, but the vulnerability of women as a social group became terribly evident. The Family Code succeeded in erasing certain historical changes that had permitted women's fuller participation in Algerian society. Algerian women were profoundly disappointed as once again the promises and dreams resulting from national liberation did not come to fruition for them.

Introduction

In April 1998, the Algerian National Assembly began debate on reforming the Family Code, a debate resulting largely from the long-time pressure of women's associations. The question of women's rights remains a taboo and delicate subject, as one element of the discussions shows clearly—that of the right to abortion, and in particular to abortion of offspring resulting from rape by Islamic terrorists. In 1998 it was estimated that since 1993 a minimum of 1,600 women had been raped and 500 impregnated by terrorists, often after being kidnapped from their homes.[16] The Haut Conseil Islamique (High Islamic Council) has yet to pronounce definitively on the right of these women to abortion, a position that has infuriated and disappointed women's groups and terrorist-victim survivors.

It is not a coincidence that the origins of the women's movement in Algeria are to be found in the early 1980s, when women rallied against the passage of the Family Code. The only true liberating force in Algeria since independence, as Mokeddem points out, has been the mass schooling of its children, including its girls.[17] Nevertheless, the paradox is that Algeria, without a doubt one of the Third World countries with the highest number of college-educated women, remains one of those that gives its women the least amount of power, status, and rights under the law.

The elites who were to restructure and rebuild Algerian society, the educational system, and the government, were almost exclusively francophone. Under colonial rule, all schooling had been done in French—this was a purposeful linguistic policy intended to disinherit the Algerians from their own language and to force them to absorb into the mainstream of French society. At the time of independence, the country thus lacked a sufficient number of qualified teachers of Arabic to move forward the policy of Arabization. To remedy this problem, thousands of mostly Egyptian and Syrian teachers were hired to teach Arabic throughout the nation's schools. The boundaries between Arabization, Islamization, and even Koranization blurred, and officially declared secularism waned as revolutionary and conservative Islam was imported into Algeria with the teachers. Under President Houari Boumédienne, the Ministry of Education was controlled by Islamists, and thus a generation of children was educated largely under Islamic principles, shaping the Algeria of today. Ironically, the mosques became one of the few places for free expression, because the FLN repressed free discussion elsewhere.

Introduction

As many of the promises made during the revolution and after liberation were not fulfilled, an increasingly angry and disillusioned populace faced the void left by the FLN and turned to the Islamists in a no-confidence vote against the FLN. The FLN's failures were many. Algeria suffered and continues to suffer from severe housing shortages, so much so that young couples must wait to be married because there are not enough lodgings outside of their parents' homes. The country does not have a sufficient number of schools or qualified teachers. There is severe unemployment, inflation, and extremely high foreign debt. The black market, the *trabendo*, flourishes.

Statistically, Algeria is a country of children—approximately 44 percent of the population is younger than fifteen years old, and 56 percent is younger than twenty.[18] A large underclass of the young has been created, keenly aware of the lack of a hopeful future; a veritable crisis of identity reigns among Algeria's young. A new word has emerged, *haittites* (in French *hittistes*), from the Arabic word *al hait,* meaning the wall. It designates "those who hold up the walls," or, loiterers: the unemployed, the marginalized, who stand around for hours with nothing to do but joke, whistle at girls, or pass the time by smoking. These are the idle and alienated young men of Algeria, and they are glaringly and menacingly present in Mokeddem's novels. In their anger, these young men and their families became the ideal target for the propaganda of the Front Islamique du Salut (Islamic Salvation Front), or FIS.[19] In the 1980s, the FIS infiltrated schools, neighborhoods, universities, and mosques, successfully offering social services the government and FLN too often failed to offer despite the clear and dire need for such services.

In the fall of 1988, the general dissatisfaction of the populace culminated in bloody riots. These were the first of the upheavals that would result in several critical events. The FLN was forced to liberalize, allowing a plurality of political parties to be created, and in Algeria's first free elections, the municipal elections of 1990, the FIS was victorious. In the December 1991 legislative elections, the FIS won the most votes, with 47.4 percent. In January 1992, the government and military staged a coup, stopped the democratic process, and annulled the elections so that power would not be taken over by the Islamists.

Some have interpreted this decision as patriotic duty, but others consider this stopping of the democratic process a historical error,

Introduction

claiming that however difficult the path to democracy might be, the vote of the people should be respected.[20] The result was violent clashes between the military and police and various militant Islamic groups. A wave of terrorist attacks followed, and President Mohammed Boudiaf was assassinated. In 1993, the attacks and bloodshed continued, and a wave of assassinations of many of Algeria's government officials and its finest intellectuals, writers, journalists, and artists began, all carried out by the FIS and other extremist groups such as the Groupe Islamique Armé (Armed Islamic Group), or GIA.[21]

At the end of the twentieth century, Algeria is still in a state of virtual civil war, as government forces continue to clash with an array of militant Islamic groups. The military designated General Liamine Zeroual as head of state, and in June 1997, legislative elections brought in a majority of moderate Islamists, some of whom have negotiated contacts with the more radical Islamist groups so as to include them in a slow process of democratization. The state has remained embroiled in a never-ending battle against the Islamic guerrilla fighters, and village massacres continue. It has been theorized that the massacres continued in part because the villagers, having formed their own militia groups to protect themselves, became rivals of the Islamic extremist groups. Furthermore, some of the latter have taken revenge on villagers and villages whom they know to have been formerly allied with other groups.

Some of the conflict has been carried to French soil; the GIA, angry at the French government for supporting the current Algerian regime, carried out terrorist attacks in 1995 and 1996, mostly in Paris. For historical, economic, and cultural reasons, France has always supported the Algerian regime, but the French government has adamantly opposed armed intervention to help end the massacres.

It is in this climate of ongoing fear, terror, and political and social turmoil that Malika Mokeddem wrote *Of Dreams and Assassins*. Mokeddem's novel is a plea, from the French side of the Mediterranean, against the violence that has left an estimated 80,000 or more civilians dead since the early 1990s.[22] Mokeddem believes that Islam is not in itself an obscurantist force but that it has been completely transformed and distorted by extremists. In her own upbringing, despite the burdens of tradition against which she rebelled, religious tolerance was the rule. She explains:

Introduction

The problem is linked to men and to political policies, . . .
a generation of children in the Fundamentalist school, that
has made the Algeria of today. . . . What hurts me the most
in Algeria today is less terrorism than school. Terrorism is an
epiphenomenon—it will pass. But the Algeria of tomorrow is
being prepared today on the school benches of the republic.
And that's the drama. It's that the mediocrity of the school
system is continuing; also, it's that with the conservative
government that was voted in and that wants to ally itself, is
allying itself with the Islamists, we can expect that to continue
anyway.[23]

In particular, Mokeddem's novel is a cry of pain at the Algerian
woman's plight in dealing with the Muslim fundamentalists at-
tempting to take away her rights in the name of the Koran:

In Muslim societies, the individual does not exist: one exists
only as a member of a tribe or clan, one does not have the
right to take initiatives. When it is a girl who takes the initia-
tive to say "I," to assert herself, to be free, it is even more dramatic. For who holds the power of tradition? Who transmits
the heritage of the absolute power of men? It is the women
themselves. So, when a girl enters school and begins to challenge this tradition that crushes everyone, the traditional family completely loses its structure, becomes panicked. This is
not the only origin of the fundamentalism surging forth here
and there, but I believe that Muslim men are very worried.
The rural exodus, immigration, unemployment, bad housing
conditions, isolation, all weaken traditional family structures
and break apart the tribe. The rebellion of a girl against her
parents is considered to be a betrayal, and the reactions are
violent. And if the girl has no support outside of the tribe, true
dramas can take place.[24]

Of Dreams and Assassins is also a settling of scores for Mokeddem and very much a "pamphleteer's novel," as she calls it. It is an
expression of great anger, and the novelist speaks of having found
a certain serenity, having finished and published this cathartic work.
In a 1997 interview she discussed wanting to write something very
different, to move away from being perceived solely as a political
novelist, constantly caught in the grip of Algeria's current events.[25]

Introduction

Her first two novels, *The Men Who Walk* and *The Century of the Locusts,* are storyteller novels, in which Mokeddem shows how strongly she is grounded in the oral tradition. They are her attempt to breathe into the French language this storytelling mode. Her second two novels, *The Forbidden Woman* and *Of Dreams and Assassins,* may be characterized as "literature of urgency," or a "literature that calls to witness."[26] She is in tune with Algerian history, and her novels represent her somewhat unusual place within Algerian society.

In Mokeddem's vision, Algerian women embody the hope for a way out of the Algerian crisis, in the same tradition as the great women fighters of the war of independence. It is not a coincidence that Mokeddem's most vivid characters are women, and educated women who know the power of learning. She has created characters who have lost everything—children, family, job, protection by the clan or tribe—and because of the ensuing despair, these women, paradoxical as it may seem, feel that they have nothing left to lose, and that they have gained strength from their experiences. She represents this profound psychological and political belief in her semi-autobiographical fiction. She comments: "And what is interesting to see is how, at the same time that women are told they are sub-human, how all of the political parties are trying to hoodwink them, to have them join in with them, because they know very well that women are the mainspring of the social change that is occurring. . . . Women have the strength of people who have nothing left to lose. Who can only win, and they will only win. They can't lose anymore. That's over with."[27]

Mokeddem's sustenance was school, education, and the world of ideas. Indeed, she claims that her "only real community is the community of ideas" and that it is impossible for her—or this novel's heroine, Kenza—either to return to Algeria or to truly fit into French society. At the heart of *Of Dreams and Assassins* is *métissage,* a French word and concept that aptly describes a mixing of cultures, languages, psychologies, and perceptions, resulting from the close association of people from different countries and backgrounds. Malika Mokeddem presents us with the possibility for, and necessity of, harmonious *métissage* in France and Algeria. The young man Slim, who becomes Kenza's friend and confidant, is half Algerian, half Malian, yet he lives with this potentially problematic racial mix with grace and an enviably carefree nature.

Introduction

In Mokeddem's *The Forbidden Woman*, the hopes for Algeria are embodied in the appealing children—the artistic and bright Dalila, who strives to reconcile society's contradictions, and Alilou, a quiet yet visionary and poetic child who is a critic of, and spokesperson for, Algeria, albeit in his own childlike manner. Hope is also expressed by the solidarity of the village women, who, like their real-life counterparts, band together and rebel. Hope in *Of Dreams and Assassins* can be found in Kenza's quest for her origins and in her ability to venture where she has no roots and nonetheless to make a new beginning. But despite the portrayal of hope in the novel, the violent and ugly realities of a society in crisis remain vivid.

In her well-known study *Anthologie de la littérature algérienne de langue française*, Christiane Achour classifies francophone Algerian literature from 1833 to 1987, both chronologically and thematically.[28] Her classifications are useful in trying to place Malika Mokeddem in the long and rich francophone Algerian literary scene, as Mokeddem is a relative newcomer, having begun writing only in the 1980s.

Achour's subdivisions take into account the following: major events in Algeria's history—in particular, the war of independence from France and independence itself; the writers' geographical location (are they in Algeria or abroad?); and the specificity of the literature—for example, women's literature and Beur literature. Achour then divides the literature into several categories. First, there is the literature written between 1948 and 1962, which she designates as works of "the soil, the nation." She treats the most classic authors of Algeria—Mouloud Feraoun, Mouloud Mammeri, Mohammed Dib, and Kateb Yacine—who write of their attachment to and love of the land, of a particular region, and their love for Algeria as a whole. This theme is explored particularly in the context of the brutal French colonial expropriation of land from the Algerians.

The war of liberation from France also inspired many writers to express the Algerians' determination to shake off colonialism's yoke. These writings are grouped by Achour into the categories of "combat writings" and "works on the war." This is true *littérature engagée,* or literature of involvement, expressing strong commitment to the cause and hope on the part of the writer, and it includes novels and witnessed accounts of the war.

Another significant category of francophone Algerian literature from 1953 to 1987 is that deriving from the emigration of Algerians to France—literature about emigration and exile. It is also the literature born from that emigration, that of the first generation of Algerians born in France, the so-called Beurs. The literature of emigration is concerned with Algeria, but naturally from a different perspective, most of it having been written in France or other western European countries.

Finally, Achour analyzes the place of the female Algerian writer from 1962 to 1987. She feels that it is necessary to treat these writers separately because they express a different reality than do male writers, that is, reflecting the condition of women in Algeria and their separate status. Achour believes there is truly a feminine voice that was able to develop in particular after the war of independence. Many of these texts are an affirmation of the feminine as something distinct, something no longer to be hidden by tradition and custom. They also represent the beginning of women's incursions into the public arena, and they tell of the fight of women in their daily lives to become equal citizens.[29]

Since 1985, many women's groups and associations have been formed whose members call for recognition of international laws governing human rights and recognition of women as autonomous and equal beings. Women have even asked for recognition of their Algerian identity before that of their Muslim identity. Women express themselves publicly more and more, and this increased freedom of expression has undoubtedly contributed to the growth of women's literary works. For the Algerian woman, writing means entering public life, affirming, expressing, and freeing herself: "Literature allows [women] to affirm an 'I' whom the rules of etiquette, customs, and traditions overshadowed. Autobiography permits them to tell of their battle, their desires, their self-promotion. Novels allow them to speak of the multiple cases, lives, and conflicts of other women, under the cover of fiction. Thus the woman is no longer confined to silence and the domestic space."[30]

Where should we place Malika Mokeddem among this array of writers? Mokeddem's themes resonate with much of Algerian literature. She too loves the land, as evidenced by the almost obsessive theme of the desert in all of her works. Mokeddem's work, in particular her third and fourth novels, is also very politically committed, as discussed above. In *The Men Who Walk*, for example, we witness the effects of the war on an Algerian family. Mokeddem

Introduction

is also a writer in exile. She chose to emigrate to France because she felt that as a woman she could not stay in Algeria. And although she initially came to France under the assumption that Algeria's political and social climate would evolve favorably, she has most certainly exiled herself because of her outspoken writings. She is clearly one of those writers whose works are born from emigration and exile and who write from the northern shore while gazing across to the south. In *Of Dreams and Assassins*, Kenza expresses her troubled feelings about exile:

> I look at the sea. A while ago still, I felt no anxiety about the northern shore. No worry about this entity called the Mediterranean. Am I also going to become, whether I like it or not, a child of the northern shore? . . . How many of us have had our memories torn apart? Our frustrations expressed or silenced? Our loves rendered painful or nostalgic? Our gaze constantly turned toward the other shore? We are affection woven between the South and the North. Cultures, memories crossbred by the North and the South. And the waves caressing Tunis, Algiers, Oran, or Tangiers give us shivers even beyond Marseilles, Montpellier, and Perpignan.[31]

Finally, Mokeddem's voice is most certainly distinctly feminine, particularly in *The Forbidden Woman* and *Of Dreams and Assassins,* novels in which the main characters are women on a quest for their identity in a society that does not give women sufficient room for self-expression. Mokeddem praises the woman whose battle is successful by freeing her from repressive traditions and customs, and she shows through her heroines that a woman can truly succeed. She shows the processes of liberation and self-promotion. Part of her pleasure and satisfaction in writing comes from her ability to show this battle to a large reading audience.

The Algerian crisis has also produced a plethora of writings—essays, poetry, drama, and novels—by Algerians living in Algeria and in exile (of which in the late 1990s there were an estimated 400,000).[32] In 1996, the exiled journalist Aïssa Khelladi cofounded, with Marie Virolle, the journal *Algérie Littérature/Action,* published monthly in Paris. The journal has received much attention from readers and writers and has become a forum for all kinds of literary and political expression about the Algerian situation. It is no coincidence that a high percentage of the manuscripts received by the journal are written by women. Indeed, in an interview in 1997,

Introduction

Aïssa Khelladi expressed his belief that women's participation will be a large part of the solution to the Algerian crisis: "It is absolutely remarkable that it is in fact women who are leading the combat, not necessarily because of a desire to be Westernized, but to escape from these laws which condemn them to second-class citizenship, which make of them children and which were promulgated by the government. . . . Nor must one forget that the demonstration of 1990, the most impressive that has ever taken place in Algeria, was a demonstration of women."[33]

At least a half dozen novels dealing with actual current events in Algeria were published by major French publishers in the late 1990s. A résumé of some of the most important can offer insight into Mokeddem's place in this wave of new literary voices. *Morituri* (Those who will die)[34] is a sometimes humorous, yet extremely grim, detective novel set in contemporary Algiers. It recounts the story of a police captain named Llob in his search for a "disappeared" woman, Sabrina Malek. The issue of the disappeared in Algeria has become a national concern, and the mothers of the unaccounted for are becoming a symbol of the Algerian crisis. Amnesty International estimated in 1996 that they numbered 10,000, but other estimates went as high as 13,000 to 14,000.[35] Honest, straightforward, and not corrupted by the "system" but actually denouncing it, Llob embodies the democratic aspirations of Algeria. *Morituri* was written by a woman under the pseudonym of Yasmina Khadra, assumed for obvious reasons of security. The author, a young woman, mother, and practicing Muslim, lives "somewhere in Algeria," keeping her exact whereabouts secret from even her European editors.[36] Khadra is a true heroine in the face of extremist fundamentalism.

More of the conditions of daily life in Algeria are recounted by Dominique Sigaud, a Frenchwoman, in *La vie, là-bas, comme le cours de l'oued* (Life down there, flowing like the wadi).[37] She witnesses and recounts the chronic fear and the way in which violence has become an everyday feature of life.

In *Sans voix* (Voiceless),[38] the main character is a woman and an artist—thus a double target for the Islamist extremists—whose husband has persuaded her to go into exile in France. In spite of her novel's title, Hafsa Zinaï-Koudil has most definitely found her voice. A television and film director in Algeria, the author of four previous novels, and the winner of the Grand Prix du Public for her film *Le démon au féminin* (The devil in female form), she be-

Introduction

lieves that women should resist through speaking, writing, and simply continuing to carry out their daily routine, even in the face of threats. It is for the above film, the true story of a woman subjected to torture under the pretext of exorcism, that Zinaï-Koudil was in 1993 condemned to death by the FIS and forced to go into exile in France.

The Islamists have clearly stated that "all of those who combat with the pen will perish by the blade." Nevertheless, Zinaï-Koudil continued her combat from France against the Islamists by writing *Sans voix*. It is a *roman-vérité*, as all of the facts cited are tragically exact—a troubling and moving book, which plunges its readers into the harrowing universe of the Algerian crisis. It is Zinaï-Koudil's voice that we hear in the first person, yet it is the larger voice of Algerian women crying out. For women are some of those most victimized by the Islamists.

Latifa Ben Mansour's *La prière de la peur* (The prayer of fear)[39] recounts the story of a woman survivor of a terrorist bomb attack in Algiers. She ends her novel with the following words, which indicate her strong belief that women are both the key to the evolution of Algerian society and the solution to Algeria's recent social and political crisis:

Under the oath of our women, fighting better than our men
You will live again, Algeria . . .
Under the oath of women,
And when they swear, they hold their promise
From your ashes, you will be reborn, Algeria.[40]

Aïssa Khelladi's *Peurs et mensonges* (Fears and lies)[41] recounts the daily existence of a journalist in hiding from the Islamists and his arrest by government media censors for publishing what is considered to be a defamatory article about the government. The novel is based largely on Khelladi's own experiences before he took refuge in France and founded *Algérie Littérature/Action*.

It is striking that several of these important works were written by women, who are in effect assuming their power through the written word. Malika Mokeddem is one of these, and her prediction that women are and will prove to have been the catalysts and "mainspring" of social change is courageously demonstrated by these women writers, all of whom put themselves at certain risk by assertively vocalizing their views and criticisms of the current Algerian situation.

Introduction

A word about style: Mokeddem does not have a feeling for dry language. If one prefers calm narrative to an overabundance of descriptive adjectives and seemingly incongruous metaphors, one might consider Mokeddem's style excessive. Yet it is difficult to put down *Of Dreams and Assassins*. To ask Mokeddem to "polish" her verbose and lyrical writing would undoubtedly be an error. For she needs fervent and intense prose to treat a subject about which she feels such passion, a subject so close to her own experiences. She needs the verbal excess to speak of the wounds of the Algerian woman who is trying to confront the bitter sorrows and the wounds of Algeria itself. Her prose has a vivid and cutting tone. She is patient and persistent, and the force of her convictions shows through. *Of Dreams and Assassins* has a sometimes breathless rhythm and indeed was written in urgency. Her anger and that of her heroine also show clearly in many short, staccato-like, clipped sentences.

Mokeddem is one of many Algerian writers who, because of historical, social, and political circumstances, writes exclusively in French. She was educated in French, and this second language has helped shape her as a writer and thinker. She has expressed great satisfaction about the fact that she writes in French. In June 1991, the French newspaper *Le Monde* published a letter written by Mokeddem titled "Langue ô ma langue" (Language, oh my language). She says about French that "it is not foreign because it vibrates in my flesh and its familiar words incessantly search through my thoughts and refine my sensibility." She claims that she is "not a hostage" of French. "[French] welcomed and took me in, a deprived child. It generously offered me the unknown shimmerings of its echoes. Whereas I was subjugated, I walked toward its enchantments." Referring to the January 1991 law calling for the exclusive use of Arab, with the goal of total Arabization by July 1997, Mokeddem concludes her letter, "If tyrants and retrograde minds fear [the French language] so much and want to forbid its use, it is because they know that it is radiant with light and always giving birth to liberty."[42]

Mokeddem's remarks about the French language are particularly relevant to current events, for the law of total Arabization, which legislates the exclusive use of Arabic for administrative affairs, in government and in teaching, went into force on July 5, 1998. The law excludes the use of French, the language of the colonizer, and Tamazight, the language spoken by the 25 percent of the Algerian population that is Berber (a politically active minor-

Introduction

ity that has fought to retain its distinct cultural and linguistic identity).[43] The law is widely predicted to fail; only a tiny minority of Algerians have mastered written Arabic, and Tamazight and French are widely spoken.

In the context of this national linguistic battle, Mokeddem's identity as a francophone writer is even more telling and significant. French, "always giving birth to liberty," gave Mokeddem access to a world beyond and separate from her ancestors and their traditions, so much of which she revolted against. She is now by definition in a battle against the unrealistic linguistic policies of Algeria. It will be fascinating to watch how she will weave into her future literary work this latest event on the Algerian political scene.

My childhood and adolescence would have been a hellish and unending imprisonment without the marvelous complicity of this language that I read in [i.e., French]. . . . For me, the desire to write is very old; it dates from adolescence. . . . For me, writing is an existential need. For a woman it is the best means of affirming her liberty; it is also a form of resistance against daily existence, which can devour you by its mediocrity.[44]

NOTES

1. *L'Humanité,* 15 April 1994, 18. My translation.
2. Quoted from my July 1997 interview with Malika Mokeddem. Translations from this interview and translations of all other quotes are mine.
3. Ibid.
4. Ibid.
5. Ibid.
6. Ibid.
7. Ibid.
8. *France Catholique,* 26 November 1993, 21.
9. Mokeddem interview.
10. Ibid.
11. Ibid.
12. Benjamin Stora, *Histoire de l'Algérie depuis l'indépendance.* Paris: Editions de la Découverte, 1994.
13. Franz Fanon, *L'an cinq de la révolution algérienne* (Paris: Maspero, 1960).
14. Mokeddem interview.
15. See Juliette Minces, *La femme voilée, l'Islam au féminin* (Paris: Calmann-Lévy, 1990), 168.
16. *L'Express,* 23–29 April 1998, 36.

Introduction

17. Mokeddem interview.
18. *L'Express,* "Spécial Algérie," 22–28 January 1998, 40–61.
19. The FIS was created in 1989. In the 1991 legislative elections, in spite of the arrest of its two founders, Abassi Madani and Ali Belhadj, the FIS obtained a majority of the votes. Following this success, the FIS was made illegal. In the late 1990s its leaders were released from prison but remained under house arrest.
20. Valéry Giscard d'Estaing, the former president of France, made this very point in an interview conducted at the beginning of 1998: "One cannot know how things would have evolved if the elections had followed their course. But this interruption was very serious, for it halted the difficult evolution toward democracy, in a country that was practically devoid of any previous references in this domain. Since then, the government has been challenged from several sides, by the left and by the Islamists. We have seen protests, demonstrations, then terrorism. This violence has hardened to the point of reaching an intolerable degree of horror" (*L'Express,* 22–28 January 1998).
21. Founded in 1992, the GIA groups together the most extreme religious terrorists in Algeria. They have claimed responsibility for almost all the assassinations of intellectuals, foreigners, and journalists; they are also responsible for the car bombings in Algiers and the massacres of villagers mostly south of Algiers, massacres only sporadically reported in the American media.
22. A 1997 article in *L'Express* estimated 80,000 deaths since 1992 ("Algérie: La 'terrible ronde barbare,' interview of Benjamin Stora, by Dominique Lagarde, 21–27 August 1997, 48–49).
23. Mokeddem interview.
24. *Le Point,* 28 August 1993, 58.
25. At the time of my 1997 interview, Mokeddem explained she was writing a more placid novel that deals with the daily lives of two Algerians living in a *qsar,* with all of the small and seemingly insignificant events that make up a life.
26. Aïssa Khelladi, an exiled Algerian journalist, used these terms in a summer 1998 interview in *La Quinzaine Littéraire:* "littérature d'urgence" and "littérature de témoignage."
27. Mokeddem interview.
28. Christiane Achour, *Anthologie de la littérature Algérienne de langue Française* (Paris: ENAP-BORDAS, 1990).
29. As the Moroccan writer Tahar Ben Jelloun says: "The word [la parole] already means taking a stand in a society that refuses the latter to women" (Jean Déjeux, *La littérature féminine de langue française au Maghreb* [Paris: Karthala, 1994], 15).
30. Déjeux, 213.
31. *Of Dreams and Assassins,* 118–19.
32. *L'Express,* "Spécial Algérie," 22–28 January 1998, 40–61.

Introduction

33. From an interview in *La Quinzaine Littéraire*, "Aïssa Khelladi: Ecrire en étranger," July 1997, 6–8.

34. The title "Those who will die" is my translation, as are the others being reviewed here. Yasmina Khadra, *Morituri* (Paris: Editions Baleine), 1997.

35. Amnesty International Country Reports, *Algeria: Fear and Silence, the Hidden Human Rights Crisis* (November 1996).

36. Guy Dugas, review of *Morituri* by Yasmina Khadra, *Le Maghreb Littéraire*, 2, no. 3, (1998): 137.

37. Dominique Sigaud, *La vie, là-bas, comme le cours de l'oued* (Paris: Gallimard, 1997).

38. Hafsa Zinaï-Koudil, *Sans voix* (Paris: Plon, 1997).

39. Latifa Ben Mansour, *La prière de la peur* (Paris: Editions de la Différence, 1997).

40. Ibid, 380.

41. Aïssa Khelladi, *Peurs et mensonges* (Paris: Seuil, 1997). First published under the pseudonym Amine Touati, in *Algérie Littérature/Action 1* (May 1996): 3–171.

42. Déjeux, 200.

43. Baki and Hugueux, "Algérie: Le Berbère et les barbares," *L'Express*, 2–8 July 1998, 37.

44. Interview in an article by Khéïra Attouche, "Passions heurtées," in *El Moudjahid*, 15 July 1992. Quoted in Déjeux, 191.

Bibliography

PRINCIPAL WORKS BY MALIKA MOKEDDEM

Les hommes qui marchent (The men who walk). Paris: Editions Ramsay, 1990. (New edition, Paris: Bernard Grasset, 1997.)

Le siècle des sauterelles (The century of the locusts). Paris: Editions Ramsay, 1992.

L'interdite (The Forbidden Woman). Paris: Bernard Grasset, 1993.

Des rêves et des assassins (Of Dreams and Assassins). Paris: Bernard Grasset, 1995.

WORKS BY MALIKA MOKEDDEM
IN ENGLISH TRANSLATION

The Forbidden Woman. Trans. and intro. by K. Melissa Marcus. Lincoln: University of Nebraska Press, 1998.

Of Dreams and Assassins

*For Abdelkader Alloula, renowned son of Oran
and of Algerian theater. ASSASSINATED.*

For Odette Marque, my French mother.

The cries of my friends grow like a reed from my tongue
Cutting into forever wounded tranquillity
I no longer know how to love
Except with this wound in my heart except with this wound
In my memory . . .
I think of friends dying without having been loved
Those judged before being listened to
I think of friends assassinated
Because of the love they knew how to pour out

I no longer know how to love except with this rage in my
    heart.
                                    —*Anna Greky,* Algérie capitale Alger

If rage were a trait from On High, I would have long ago
transcended my status as a mortal.
                                    —*Cioran,* Aveux et anathèmes

                                    (Confessions and curses)

Emptiness and Excess

Long before my birth, something was already out of kilter in my family. My father already had his own illness, sex. He must have caught it at puberty. It seems that he was driven out by his own people for this reason. It's true that the moment you see him, you can tell he's a man continually on the prowl. He hunts down indiscriminately. Skirts, haiks, veils . . . Age doesn't matter. Neither do family ties.

When there are no women around, he dreams about them. Gluttonously. Huddled up, he burps and purrs. Pushes his turban back to the top of his skull. Scratches his forehead. Moves a feverish hand over his entire body, plunges it to the bottom of his baggy ankle-length *serwal*. His eyes roll upward. His mustache quivers.

As a child, I observed him discreetly. Often. And often without wanting to, I caught him screwing the neighbor women.

Now he's nothing more for me than a caricature.

My mother . . . I never knew her. My earliest childhood is marked as much by her absence as by my father's excesses. Emptiness and excess. Two huge opposites without balance.

I was still in her womb when my mother took the boat for France. It was in 1962, at the time of Algeria's independence. They'd married her off a year earlier. Against her will, obviously.

I was inside her. She was in the throng of the *pied-noir*

exodus. Not for the same reasons as they. Her brother, impris-oned during the war because of his activities in the FLN, had just been released in Montpellier. His health was in such an impaired state that it was said he was dying.

My mother was sent to take care of him. I was born then.

When our country's independence came, everyone partici-pated in the revelry. My father too. In his own way. While his wife was taking care of her brother and bringing me into the world in Montpellier, he took up his own habits. In five months' time, he had taken and repudiated a wife. For unruli-ness. In the meantime, since he had impregnated the maid, he married her too. At least she was submissive. Even grate-ful. Unmarried mothers experience much suffering, of course! With her, my father could continue to indulge in his excesses without a fuss.

As soon as her brother was better, my mother returned to Oran. Found her maid pregnant. She didn't even unpack her bundle of things. She took off again immediately. Alone. I was three months old when my father grabbed me from her arms on a doorstep.

Besides the neighbors, and willing or downtrodden women found by chance in the streets, my father had at his disposal the female clientele at his butcher shop. And among them the widows of martyrs.

A rumor had spread during those first days of freedom: "We cannot let war widows remain alone for very long. To remedy this calamity, it is a man's duty to take six wives." In our coun-try, arrogance makes males blind to the ridiculous.

As for my father, his sexual voraciousness couldn't be trou-bled with legitimacy. Polygamy was nothing but a restriction to him. Without ever being in the Maquis or the resistance, he had finally discovered a "national contribution" to his liking: an enthusiastic campaign for the repopulation of Algeria. In his eyes, even heroism and patriotism were inseparable from fornication.

His obsession was an ideal activity in an ideal setting: the butcher shop. Between suspended animal carcasses, among swarms of flies, and with the odor of blood, he is at ease. Handling meat keeps him ready while he waits for prey. You have to see him grab hold of a large piece of beef or mutton, and with a wrestler's movement, throw it onto the butcher's block. He grabs an ax and whack! whack! whack! three chops, three breaths. Cut up. He moves away. Fascinated, he observes the scene: gaping cuts, crushed bones. He takes a large kitchen knife and returns to the attack. Spreads apart, delves into the flesh. Sucks his fingers. Clicks his tongue. He has no concept of skilled carving. He couldn't care less about the pieces of bone, the gashed slices. Only contact with the flesh counts. He doesn't prepare it, he grabs hold of it, hacks it, kneads it, manhandles it. Then gets rid of it by throwing it in a heap onto some newspaper. Rolls the whole thing into a ball. The paper is dampened. Rings blur and wipe out the letters. My father stares at these stains with an expression of silent amusement bordering on lunacy. Lunacy that gets the best of him as soon as a woman crosses the threshold of his shop.

Women are nothing more than meat to him. What's more, with the most destitute of his clientele, my father excels at barter: a bit of lamb, mutton, or camel in exchange for sex. Beef is too expensive.

His first son was born eleven months after me. As the years went by, my father and his wife inflicted six brothers and two sisters on me, half siblings . . . but legitimate. In the building there were, however, always one or two other children who resembled them so much that it was disconcerting. I wasn't alone in my surprise. After hearing a thing or two from some vengeful tongue, our most naive neighbors ended up with concrete proof.

The scenario of hostilities between my father and them was always the same. To start with, a few infringements and angry outbursts. Then the conflict became more firmly entrenched, expanded, and exploded. Men, women, and children living in the building would split into two camps. They would join the melee. Some would shout jubilantly: "Men who marry whores get what they deserve. It's the duty of a man worthy of what he's got in his pants to make the most of his good luck and even to seek it out!" Others were indignant with "the scoundrel who betrays their trust, befouls his own dignity and theirs." A generalized brawl marked the height of the confrontations. The building then took on the appearance of a ship ravaged by mutiny. Smashed doors. Showers of insults. Death threats. Blows of truncheons, of cans, chairs, knives . . . Everything inside of the apartments was turned into a war arsenal.

Yet no judicial complaint was ever brought against him. These stories are worked out in private, behind walls. It's a question of honor! The hullabaloo of beatings was followed by that of repudiations and neighbors moving out. Then, suspicion spreading, a silence fell on the building. The children even became afraid of the sound of their steps in the staircase. As if each one were aware that the slightest creaking noise could be like a match in a haystack.

So we often got new neighbors. Which was not displeasing to my father, who, as soon as his wounds were healed, began to swagger again, ogling the new female tenants.

My father never loved me. I really got back at him for that. I was gifted with a look that made him angry. I tolerated him even less when he was shouting. So I yelled even louder than he did. Very early I learned the power of my yelling. Girls and women who raise their voices terrorize him. Make him beat a retreat.

I yelled so that he would not consider me as the "maid of his maid," his sons' scapegoat. I yelled when I perceived his greedy eyes fixed on my legs, my neck, my hips. I yelled from disgust. Yelling kept hideous reality at bay.

In the face of the abyss opening inside of me, I would yell in panic, and often.

But as soon as I was far away from him, uncontrollable

Of Dreams and Assassins

giggles that dismayed others took hold of me. Giggles that shook me, that exacerbated my fears. Maybe I laughed excessively? The others decreed: "She's really crazy." And they left me alone.

During school breaks my father would get rid of me by sending me to his brother's home in the desert. How many fiery furnaces did I endure? About fifteen, at least. My fear of the desert's immensity was always swept away by the joy of leaving my family. And, until I was nine years old, by a joy just as great at seeing my whimsical friend, Alilou, once again. Alilou! I was no older than four when I first met him. He at once intrigued me. In that world that was like a dream, people move around slowly. With broad movements. As if floating. But Alilou, dark and slender, ran around babbling all day long. As for me, I stood still at the foot of a palm tree. I watched him. I still have these memories from my stays in the Sahara: people with expressive gestures, slowed by the weight of silence and the vastness of the horizon. And there was Alilou running like a sylph of light.

One morning he came toward me:

"Come along!"

"Where?"

"On my sputnik. We're going to burst through the sky and go to the stars."

What a plan, to burst through the sky! I followed him, walking. After a moment he turned around in exasperation. Came back toward me. He took my hand to pull me along at his speed. Alilou was the only therapy for my childhood . . . To my great sorrow, my friend disappeared one day. He abandoned me to the terrible confinement I felt in the desert. One thing is certain, though. In that place, battling the elements of the cosmos, I attached no more importance to my father's escapades than to dogs frolicking. There, in the desert, life oscillates between flashes of anguish and vast expanses of lethargy. There, the summers bite into the winters and, with a few angry attacks of the sand wind, assassinate all of spring's vague desires. There, each summer is a death by incineration. Even melancholy is subject to summer's cremation. Even light turns into summer's ashes. Only the dates seem to thrive. They become golden brown and gleam like little clusters of suns that mock the children. For a long time. Finally, they become amber colored, ripen, and fall. Fall like big drops of warm honey. They rain, shining and sweet, on burned desires. Only then does the torpor yield. The flies come. And it's back to school.

Hurrah! Back to school! It saves me from the desert and my family.

As soon as I could manage on my own, it is I who fled from my father, his bestiality, his complaining horde of brats, his wife-servant, the atmosphere of the apartment building, which had become suffocating. At the end of primary school, I got a scholarship that opened the doors of a boarding school to me. Making me like all school children. The country's independence had created advantages other than those my father asserted for himself.

The El Hayat Lycée was my first refuge. El Hayat: life. Life in this former convent was narrow and cemented in. Endlessly rising walls. A fragment of sky . . . But these barriers were also protective. For the passing years had brought me other enemies: my half brothers. I pitted my calmness against their despotism. Put up other walls between them and me. Walls of all our differences surrounded by my silence. In behaving this way, I committed an injustice to Lamine. He was a good student, and his reflective disposition was surprising in the midst of the bragging and tyranny of the others. But, hardened by my isolation and resistant to any family ties, I didn't make a distinction between him and the others.

Left to their own devices, the boys were repeatedly expelled from school. Dragging each other along, they joined the wave

of loiterers, the guys "holding up the walls." They roamed
the city like ferocious guards. I hid away in the lycée.

Huddled in my solitude, I watched the other girls. I could
make out only a bustling, chattering flock that took off from
the lycée each weekend. I couldn't detect any particular savagery toward me in their mockery. It was so symbolic of a
moral strength I lacked that I was even envious of it. To my
mind, their savagery lay in words that usually suggested affection: father, mother, brothers, sisters . . . but which, in this
case, were nothing more than puffs of air.

I didn't leave the lycée. Not even for holidays. Or only long
enough to do a few errands or to go to the house of Combes,
my French teacher. Enjoying the silence, in a lycée emptied of
its boarders, was too precious to me. A privileged time for
reading. Sometimes, in the midst of a story, I seemed to meet
Alilou. And I repeated to myself these words said by a wise
man from his oasis: "Alilou is not dead. He has left for the
realm of eternal childhood."

In the summer, I always managed to find some job in order
to escape from the house again and to be able to buy myself
some books, a nourishment essential for loneliness.

It seems that my mother took me away during one of her
returns to Oran. My father apparently combed the city for
two weeks and beat up his wife. It seems that I was found at
the foot of the apartment building the day my mother took
the boat again for France. I was two years old. It seems that,
subsequently, all her efforts to see me again were in vain. Did
my father have antennae? Did she come again to demand me
at his shop? I do not know. When I was in elementary school,
my father pulled me out on three occasions, under what pretext I didn't know, to take me for a few days to visit people he
knew. Never the same ones. Always away from the city. Once,
he left me with a family for an entire month.

At those times, I was so overwhelmed that I forgot about yelling and began to cry. I was studious and already conscious of the school's role in rescuing me.

"If you keep crying, you'll never set foot in school again!"

Terrorized by this threat, I shut up. I discovered later, much later, that these somber periods coincided with my mother's passing through Oran. One question obsessed me: Why hadn't she taken me away that first time? What I sensed completely paralyzed me. It was a terrible thought that my mind could neither admit nor express.

One day, a little neighbor child slipped inside our house and whispered to me:

"There's a woman waiting for you in the street. She wants to talk to you about your mother."

I rushed outside. The unknown woman squeezed me in her arms. Wiped away tears with her veil:

"My little Kenza, come with me. Your mother has died. Did your father tell you?"

I shook my head no. She continued:

"We brought her body back from Montpellier two days ago. She was buried this morning. I want to show you her grave."

It must have been a Thursday, because I didn't have classes. My father must have been at the butcher shop, so the coast was clear. I followed the woman. She hailed a taxi. We got in.

I remember the feeling of unreality that took hold of me. I remember the odor of orange blossoms pervading the air. I remember the invasive light from the sun. A sky imbued with blueness. It was springtime. I was eight years old.

At the cemetery the woman stopped at the burial mound of a freshly dug grave and said:

"This is your mother."

Since I remained unresponsive, she took a picture out of her bag and handed it to me:

"Here she is. This is your mother."

I saw a very young face that smiled up at me. My feeling of

Of Dreams and Assassins

unreality became even stronger. I had never seen these features tremble. Had no memory of a kiss, no fragment of a shared life to thus give life to this word: mother. The absence of an unknown woman. The face in the picture changed nothing. I couldn't lose a mother whom I had never had. Nor feel vicarious sadness. I had to make an effort not to burst out laughing and offend the woman. For her pain intimidated me and excluded me even more.

As she accompanied me back home, she gave me a bit of money and said to me:

"You're too young . . . In a few years I'll tell you about your mother. Come see me in Montpellier when you're older. I won't see you again here. Even out of faithfulness to Keltoum's memory, I wouldn't want to have anything to do with your father. Don't forget, my name is Zana Baki."

As an adolescent, I sometimes overheard my stepmother whispering to her women neighbors or close relations. I knew it was about my mother. As soon as they saw me they all hushed up. In those staring eyes, I could detect only blame toward the deceased woman. Then they lowered their eyes. I didn't try to find out what they were talking about. Might as well keep my ignorance and this unsullied silence.

And besides, I had no taste for misfortune. Since I was always immersed in scandal or melodrama, I had acquired a certain capacity for indifference. That protected me from the worst.

Sometimes I went to the cemetery without managing to persuade myself that my mother was there, underground. That the absent woman was dead. The feeling of her absence, little by little, was dying in me. I became disinterested in this place and sank into forgetfulness. A few months later, I didn't find Alilou in the desert. He too had disappeared. From that time on, I could expect nobody. And in the loss of expectation, I certainly lost a little of myself, too.

After that, I began to laugh even harder. To laugh about everything. To laugh in order to chase away my nightmares. To laugh so as not to be overwhelmed. Soon my laughter had more effect than my yelling. I realized this at the lycée, where

Of Dreams and Assassins

the girls remained petrified whenever I laughed in their faces. I think they'd nicknamed me "the Drill." Or maybe I'm the one imagining it, since I felt that my laughter pierced them. I don't know any longer. Whatever the case may be, I stopped yelling.

Without a doubt, laughter deprived me of hatred and the surge of energy it brings. Deprived of this force, I sank further and further into indifference.

For a long time I thought that indifference was an expression of the greatest despair. Despair healed by amputating a part of oneself. The best part. What is left is a weakness that paralyzes you. Blinds you. Keeps you locked up. Now I wonder if this state actually requires an even stronger will than hatred. That is, perhaps it is the greatest violence inflicted on others by extreme self-control. A cold passion, closed in on itself because it has no purpose . . . I don't know. And anyway, what do explanations matter. They never change any part of reality.

Most girls, born as I was at the time of Independence, were named Houria: Liberty; Nacira: Victory; Djamila: the Beautiful One, a reference to the Djamilas who were war heroines . . . Me . . . I was named Kenza: Treasure. How ironic! I had none of life's treasures. Not even the affection a child deserves. This first name suits me as little as those applied to shackled Liberties, enslaved Victories, and scorned heroines. Quite soon, I realized what a paradox this was. And I soon understood that it was from neither sadism nor cynicism that we were given these first names. Ignorance is unaware of its own perversions.

Maybe we would have known right away what to expect if we had been given names such as Scorned, Undesirable, Ill-Loved . . . and Treasure of Ruin.

School—the only glimpse of another world. Learn the language of the other, first steps toward originality. Toward a deeper and deeper solitude. And each time the school year began again, I discovered that fathers had pulled out some Hourias, Naciras, and Djamilas from school to marry them off, by force. I should have suspected something! I should never have believed that this immense collective dream of liberty, which excited everyone, was going to contribute to the forming of different men. It already carried within itself its own discriminations. Fathers who shatter the futures of their own daughters are capable of enslaving all freedom.

Something was already out of kilter in the country as soon as Independence came. But I didn't know that yet.

The Unexpected and the Worst

One Saturday afternoon, when I was in my last year at the lycée, Lamine, the oldest of my father's sons, showed up in front of the gates. He stated his name and asked to see me. A monitor had him brought into the visiting room and let me know he was there. Never before had anyone visited me at the boarding school. So I immediately suspected some serious reason. Perhaps my father's death? Had someone killed him? Intrigued, I headed toward the courtyard and came to a halt a few steps from Lamine.

"Here, I've brought you this."

With neither a hello nor any preliminaries, Lamine handed me two books: *As I Lay Dying* and *The Stranger.* The choice of these two titles left me even more dumbfounded than his visit. How had Lamine succeeded in guessing so well? I thought that he and I were as different as Camus and Faulkner. Relatively speaking! Disconcerted, I looked at the books and didn't dare admit to him that I had already read them. Nor did I dare to thank him.

After a moment of embarrassment, we went toward a bench and sat down in silence. Lamine had a puzzled look and, staring at the ground, said:

"Even when a person is incapable of feeling affection for humans, there are books to love. I'm sure that these two will move you."

" . . . "

"Incapable of feeling affection for humans." Was he speaking about himself or about me? I didn't ask.

Of Dreams and Assassins

"Do you think you're the only one in the world who feels despair? Look around you once in a while."

He had murmured the last sentence like a plea. His hands were trembling a little.

"I can understand that you hate my father . . . "

Offended by this verb, I couldn't stop myself from crying out:

"I don't hate him, he's so grotesque! I couldn't care less about him, that's all!"

"That's worse . . . But my mother, what has she done to you?"

" . . . "

"She took the place of yours? Her or another one, what difference does it make? Women have no control over what happens."

"They have everything to do with it. They are accepting."

"Not your mother in any case! She rebelled. She decided to leave, to leave everything. She chose. She must have been a courageous woman . . . Mine is a victim and will remain so, like so many other women. Victim of an entire education and of ignorance, you know that!"

" . . . "

He glanced at me. A strange light lit up his face. Exasperation or discouragement in the face of my silence? He lowered his head.

"You're ill from solitude, and you've never done anything to get out of it! On the contrary, you lock yourself in more and more. Something's not right with you."

I've heard that so many times. With the years I've been able to persuade myself that if "something" had come apart in me, it's because our world engenders its own failures, devastation, barbarity . . . I'm just one of those most susceptible to its damage. You manage as best you can. And during adolescence, you still have some resources left intact.

"You never talk. Not even about your mother. It's as if nothing gets to you."

" . . . "

"When I was nine years old, I saved up money for months. I went without comics, candy, and even movies. I wanted to get you a present for your tenth birthday. I won't tell you how anxious I was as the date approached. I didn't have enough money to pay for what I coveted. I was reduced to going through my father's pockets while he napped. A wasted effort. Are you kidding, that clever guy never falls asleep without putting his change under the pillow! So I went to the store to swipe it from his cash register. When I finally had the money, and I think I would have done anything to get it, I bought a doll that seemed so beautiful to me. The most beautiful doll in the world. Do you remember what you said to me when I held it out to you?"

I shook my head.

"So you don't remember!"

He remained quiet for a moment before continuing.

"You said: 'What the hell do you want me to do with a doll?' with such an indifferent look. My mother grabbed it from my hands and put it on the TV. Two or three days later, insane with rage, I took it back and ran and threw it into the sea."

He was quiet for a long time. He ran his hands nervously through his mop of hair. He crossed and uncrossed his legs and clenched his hands on the edge of the bench. He jumped onto his feet all of a sudden and with suppressed anger said:

"Pardon me for having dared bother you."

Took a few steps. Stopped and turned around:

"Happy birthday anyway!"

He shrugged his shoulders with a half smile that just as quickly left his face when he saw the books against my chest. His look made me aware that I had grabbed them, that they had been lying on the bench, and I was hugging them in my arms. Transformed, Lamine hesitated a moment.

"If you need me, write to me at the lycée. Maybe it's easier to write than to speak."

Then he left, passing quickly through the gates and disappearing into the street. I didn't move from the bench. I'd forgotten my birthday, as usual. My seventeen years were an eternity that lasted an instant. Time crumbled. As I stared at

Of Dreams and Assassins

the ironwork of the gate, I thought again of Lamine's words. Why hadn't he told me about the sacrifices he'd made for that purchase? As for me, I was so firmly convinced that I existed for no one! Maybe I would have been completely changed by what he'd done. Maybe I would have learned to love if I had gathered some proof of affection. Or was I so closed in on myself as to be blind to others? I don't know . . .

My memory is made up of sensations interrupted by big black holes. And if I had no memory of Lamine's gesture, suddenly I could clearly see the doll sitting on the television. It had seemed to me then that she had landed there like a guest too fancy for our shack. That her eyes and her smile had frozen in place with disdain at the spectacle of our life. It's true that, to my great relief, I didn't have to tolerate her for very long.

I was happy to own these two books. I'd be able to reread them whenever I wanted to. I had borrowed them from the lycée library the first time. I caught myself caressing them distractedly. Had Lamine turned sixteen? I doubted it. I could see his child's look through the haze of what I had forgotten and my rejections. As if I had only just discovered it. He already carried the mark of that fate which sometimes strikes in childhood: lucidity. It gave him a painful intensity. How could I have not noticed it? How could I have not seen that the world's dissonance had left troubled echoes in him, too? Wasn't I a rotten little bitch preoccupied solely with her own pain? Pain that was carefully nurtured in silence so as to make it stand out more? Pain displayed so as to permanently and indiscriminately accuse all of my family?

I felt as shaken as I was helpless. For the first time.

It took me more than a month to get over this intrusion into my isolation. It was obvious that Lamine's words had cut an opening in my armor. Their echo plunged me into endless dreams out of which I emerged spirit and body broken.

Of Dreams and Assassins

Dreams resembling long walks at the end of which you're overtaken by exhausted drunkenness. At times I caught myself smiling. I glanced around me as if I'd been caught in an act of wrongdoing. One day while studying, my hand began to write: my brother, my brother, my brother . . . In a childish style that in no way resembled my usual handwriting. The quavering of this tirelessly repeated word expressed without a doubt the battle between my will and an irrepressible surge toward Lamine that had emerged from I don't know where. Something never felt before. I gave birth to this word against my will. I don't know which one of us, he or I, tried in vain to tame the other.

After a moment I found myself feeling so stupid that my furor took over. I lifted my pen from the paper. And after thinking, I finally concluded that what was bringing me closer to Lamine was a crisscrossing of our feelings of helplessness. Of two states of solitude. Of two silences plunged in human turmoil. Deposits left by reading . . . Blood ties had no part in it. On the contrary. The nausea I experienced from just hearing the word "family" had separated us since our youngest age. That word had made Lamine even more of a stranger to me than any unknown person. This acknowledgment saved me. Placed Lamine outside the field of my silences and my conflicts. I ripped out the page of my notebook, crumpled it with the feeling that I was crushing this word, brother, like an empty shell. And cheerfully threw it into the garbage.

Hopping out of bed the next morning, and before washing my face, I scribbled on a sheet of paper: "And how about going for a walk together?" I hastily put it in an envelope.

Split between the fear of a new meeting and the obsessive fear that Lamine wouldn't come, I impatiently waited for the end of the week. Lamine was at the lycée gates Saturday afternoon.

I joined him. We began to walk side by side.

Of Dreams and Assassins

Usually when I left the lycée, I did not look around me at
either the people or the city. Distracted, I would scurry down
Boulevard Lescur to the SNED bookstore. I would spend a
long time leafing through beautiful books. Nosing around in
search of new things to read. My purchases made, I would go
toward the oceanfront. There, leaning on the railing, I would
admire the shimmering water and the freighters anchored in
the harbor. I could never dream there for very long nor ex-
tend the sight of the ocean by my memory of the desert. Very
quickly, an intruder would show up, for whom the view of a
girl alone and motionless, facing the sea, was a pressing invitation to lust. In the street, even dreaming is forbidden to us.
Immediately sullied.

Vexed, I would return to the boarding school and close myself in, to travel and dream as I wrote. In paper secrets.

But in Lamine's company I began to look around at store
windows, walls, balconies, café terraces . . . Was it that the
city was finally beginning to exist because of Lamine's presence? Did the latter set me free from the fear brought on by
the crowds? Or was it my way of indicating to Lamine, by
resolutely hiding my face, that I had no desire to talk? Without a doubt, it was a combination of all of that. Besides, hands
in pockets, Lamine didn't look at me either. Didn't speak
to me. We contented ourselves with moving forward together
amidst the crowd.

It was from that moment on that I became conscious of my
effort not to meet the eyes of others.

Crisscross the city that way. Stroll along the coast road.
Climb up toward Santa Cruz . . . We said nothing to each other,
or almost nothing. We were two parallel states of ennui. At
once together and alone. A tacit agreement preserved a fragile balance between us. Our mutual attraction-repulsion was
thus rendered harmless. Our misfortunes appeased.

But we exchanged books. Without comment. Yet the choice
of books was never insignificant. It implicated us. Altogether,
we had a dialogue with reading as the intermediary. Through

Of Dreams and Assassins

the words of authors who brought us together without clashes or constraint.

Only at the end of a few months did we express ourselves with words. As if, during this time, we had advanced not side by side but one toward the other. As if all the kilometers covered, all the weariness felt, all the pages read had been as many paths toward an unsuspected goal, the true encounter. The communion of ideas. I was the first one to speak. We were walking by the sea. Maybe the sea prompted me to speak of Alilou, the brown angel who carried within him the excesses and the light of the desert. I recounted his imaginary world, his disappearance, and my pain. And this atrocious feeling that all of the children of the world, and insouciance, had disappeared with him.

I also owe to these walks the discovery of my city. I owe to them the happiness, now in ruins, of having discovered it before it was totally disfigured by rural exodus, misery, and obscurantism.

Boulevard Lescur: Elysée Couture, clothes imported who knows how. Exorbitant prices. The jumble of the Bata department store. Hotel Timgad, formerly the Café Riche. Show-off luxury. Raoul and Bailly, for which the only tributes paid are those for their foreign names. Local production? A swindle that bangs around on your feet by the end of a few days and creates prosperity for the shoe repairmen. There are many of these.

The Place d'Armes: in the center, the statue of the emir, crushed by his own ambition. The city hall's bronze lions adorning the entryway. In the foyer, an orderly: ignorance clad in self-sufficiency. Since Independence, everyone here wants to be a leader. A national longing. What can a man who crushes only his wife take pride in? Shame on him! And in this race for privileges, idiocy always wins. Ethics and intelligence take a firm last place. People also take a wicked pleasure in letting others cool their heels and in humiliating those who have the misfortune of showing the resulting scars. "Keep in line! Wait your turn!" Unless you're the friend, the cousin, or the sister

of somebody higher up, you find yourself standing in a line for
no reason. Obtaining even the most routine papers turns into
a veritable obstacle course, punctuated with closed counter
windows and bureaucrats who are ignoramuses. While orderlies sit like monarchs on their thrones at wobbly tables in the
midst of drafts, citizens waste their time.

Across from the city hall is the officers' mess hall. Military
stripes and clothing creases as rigid as their minds. Next door,
a small dead-end street curves round and overlooks the shoals
of Sidi El Houari. One day, when we'd reached the end and
were turning around to go back, we heard:
"Watch out!"
In front of us, a few drops of water were dripping from a
balcony. We looked up.
On the third floor of an opulent apartment building, a
woman in a low-cut dress, arms bare, was watering geraniums.
She spoke to us apologetically:
"They're so thirsty!"
A smile lit up her tanned face. She had hair as dark as night
and big, light-colored eyes highlighted with eyeliner.
Madame Ibanez! I knew her by name. Knew she lived on
this dead-end street. Lace, silk, velvet, lamé—all of the fabric
of the elegant women of Oran passes through her hands. Apparently, Madame Ibanez has a date-book that is always full.
An appointment is required long in advance to use her services. So I had seen her eyes and her smile! They dazzled me.
I looked up again. She had disappeared. This woman was quite
obviously more Oranian than I was. She participated in what
made Oran's reputation: the city of all pleasures and the gentle
way of life. The thought made me burst into laughter. Lamine
turned toward me and anxiously observed me.
Boulevard Soummam, formerly Gallieni. A handicrafts
shop. Air Algérie. The Café Cintra, a red velvet cocoon huddled behind its windows where men took refuge to have a little
drink in peace. Then the terminal for buses going to the beach,
facing the Lycée Pasteur, in front of which always paraded a
crowd of *tshitshis:* French students and children of noteworthy

Of Dreams and Assassins

Algerians who had the privilege of attending this establishment. Then we returned to Arzew Street . . .

Back then, the city was clean and peaceful. The streets full of girls in jeans, with miniskirts and wild hair. The most brazen or courageous of them dared to sit at the tables of a café terrace and protested loudly if they were refused service. At that time, we were divided only into Algé-Rois and Algé-Riens. And the majority of the "Nothings" and the less-than-nothings, the women, still managed to put up with the pretentions of a few "Kings." Back then, the Algé-Rois still scorned our *raï*, but showed up in packs each weekend, because Oranian women were attractive. Back then, from balcony to balcony, the old women nostalgically exchanged lengthy tirades with one another in Spanish. We weren't yet ashamed of our cultural crossbreeding. That would come later. Back then, even veils were sexy. White, with just enough transparency to let the miniskirt, pants, or long dresses with slits show through. More opaque, they brought out the essence of sensual turmoil and lit up the imagination. And the women wearing them would all of a sudden move from side to side on their high heels as their titillated suitors called them "my dove." Dove. They were thus celebrated by performers of *raï, sha'abi*, Andalusian music, and the Bedouin flute, who, nevertheless, made it a point of honor to royally ignore each other. Back then, wine was still flavorful and inexpensive. And to accompany it, students would drive all the way to Aïn El Turc, on the coast, to buy provisions of pork from the celebrated pork butcher, Sorriano.

Back then, we were proud of the *pied-noir* brothers who had stayed on. And of our hospitality offered to any foreigner. That was before the demented wave of hatred. Before the hysteria of the Kalachnikovs and the funeral trance of knives. Before the *fatwas* calling for rape.

Of Dreams and Assassins

Now terror and the forbidden burn everything to ashes. The city hall's famous lions have lost their fangs. The leprous manes and bodies seem to be gnawed away by the evil that is devouring life and the city. Now Sorriano's delicatessen is an office of the FIS. Sacrilege! Now, adding to the division between "Kings," "Nothings," and less-than-nothings, there are "isms" and other upheavals devastating the country. Now laws go further than tradition. They've left women without any rights at all. Intelligence is no longer just a scarecrow that makes concierges and orderlies act, but is a crime. And under this reign of bastards, Algeria has become the stage for all possible disgraces: girls raped in front of their parents. Stolen and taken away to the Maquis, where blood-thirsty monsters, their rut satisfied, mutilate and dispose of them. Poor crumbs of their savagery. *Pieds-noirs,* who'd stayed here for the love of their country, more Algerian than us, were murdered for confirming the risk of birth by choice. Now, rifles and daggers in hand, they're bleeding us of our otherness. Our legendary hospitality has become a macabre legend. Become a hunt for the foreigner. One's features are a crime. And so many features are held in contempt that I am afraid. Afraid of the terror that prowls. That sows suspicion all the way to the hearts of families. Afraid for my friends, for the women, the little girls, the thinkers, the unknown like Madame Ibanez, who has never sewn dresses for me. Now, the *entchadorées* resemble crows. The bearded or hooded, like the enraged fanatics of the Ku Klux Klan, decimate the country. And we . . . we have nothing left but enemies! For the *ninjas,* who are supposed to protect the people, are worried only about defending the privileges of the army and the Mafia caste, unwilling to lose the reins of power. And to rob them of this power, the fundamentalists would like to assassinate the very soul of this people and its pluralistic identity. And we who wanted a democracy! Our people have their throats slit like sheep for the *L'aid* or they fall to bullets because they dare demand secularity. Demand that religion prove it is tolerant. That faith recognize human rights, including the right to be an atheist.

By what perversion did the generation of Independence become transformed into hordes of alienation and death?

Of Dreams and Assassins

Now all sorts of sirens wail all day long in the disaster-stricken city. So goes the world under Allah's skies. Skies whose blue is cruelty itself. It takes offense at nothing. Carries no cloud of human destruction. Makes radiant the lies of nonexistent peace and joy.

Now, there are moments when I really feel crazy enough to scream.

Sinful Love

I thought my father's sexual insanity had made me immune to carnal love. Believed myself at least too repulsed, if not frigid, to give in to it. Told myself that without a doubt Platonic love would offer me a refuge. Well, no. I did it. With an ardor that I didn't know was in me. I allowed the forbidden into my bed. All of my most ardent thirst. Felt my skin open to the flow of desire. My body gorge itself with pleasure. And surprise swept it away.

Once the initial ecstasy was over, even banality suddenly had a fearful attraction, and my past seemed to me a long period of shedding that I abandoned without regret.

Lamine, who for several days had been observing me with amused curiosity, teased me:

"My word, it's love at first sight!"

"Love at first sight?"

"Look at yourself in a mirror!"

Looking at myself was something I hadn't stopped doing. It was as if my body was taking its revenge on my denials and what it had been deprived of. It was escaping me. I reared up and boasted.

"No, not love at first sight."

"You're right. You were incinerated. Now you're glowing. You're more a sudden light!"

I burst out laughing.

"Yeah, listen, even your laughter has lost its sarcasm. Now it's radiant. Haven't you noticed?"

"No."

Of Dreams and Assassins

I stared suspiciously at Lamine. Was he provoking me? I wasn't sure, despite his mocking smile. My laughter was my only weapon! Had I become that vulnerable? My mouth hung open in surprise.

Was this force that hurled me toward Yacef "a burst of light"? That transformed my being and its relationship to the world? This strange stirring in the deepest part of my soul. This fire running through my flesh. I who was so afraid of others' eyes, who never looked at them in order to keep myself out of reach, I began looking feverishly for Yacef's eyes. In the same way that one exposes oneself to the spring sun's rays to rid oneself of winter shivers.

And how ironic to approach love with desire. Snatched up by passion, I entered into its mystery without giving up my doubts. The force of what was happening to me rang like an alarm. Grappling with these paradoxes, I felt as if I were on a high wire stretched between anxiety and delight. All I had done was turn my back on humanity's sordidness. But I knew that it was always there, ready to mow me down. Love was staggeringly dangerous, and I found myself powerless in the face of it. Dispossessed of my indifference, of its cynical outbursts and its sardonic laugh. Lost in my contradictions. Delightful distress.

Love was proof against all thirst. And unbeknown to me, I was also slowly opening up to others, finally discovering warmth and friendship, the sense of sharing and of celebration. Even my relationship with Lamine increased in intensity. In warmth, in complicity.

It was my first year at the university. As for my studies, I might have ended up in a catastrophic situation if I hadn't regained my self-control at the very last minute. This honeymoon of the senses almost cost me a diploma.

I lived in campus housing. Yacef lived with his parents.

Oranian bourgeois, whom he said were very conservative. Who isn't in Algeria? That didn't prevent us from spending the better part of our time together. To diminish his family's scoldings, Yacef rarely spent the night, waiting for me to doze off before leaving. One afternoon while we were walking on the coastal road, going toward Canastel, he said to me:

"You know, my parents are convinced they can marry me to a little cousin from Algiers. In spite of my protests, the poor girl has been taken out of high school to prepare her trousseau."

We laughed about it together. Not for an instant did the idea that this kid could represent any danger trouble my mind. Love's certainties had almost swept away my doubts. And my apprehensions. Even allowed me a little compassion for the fate, alas so common, of this child.

Yacef was certainly a son of the upper middle class. He was one of the few students to own a brand-new car. A very rare thing here where most of our vehicles are nothing but scrap heaps that still run thanks to the virtuosity and resourcefulness of the local mechanics.

Yacef had shown me his house. A fortress with bars on the windows and the shutters always closed. It seemed so much a luxurious prison to me that the sight of it gave me shivers. Arguing that the modesty of one's social condition must soften personalities, I ended up wishing that Yacef came from a poor family. But just the thought of my father made me change my mind, tell myself that one's origins, whatever they may be, have never kept men from insane behavior and going downhill.

*　*　*

Once our studies were over, both of us got jobs as *maîtres-assistants* at the Faculté des Lettres. And after a fight with the university administration, I wrestled from them the right to a small faculty apartment.

It had been such a long time since I'd gone near my father's place. The excuse of my studious life, incompatible with the atmosphere of the house, was convenient for everyone. He had allowed my first stay in the boarding school and then in university housing. And even if the latter had the reputation of being a place of moral depravity, at least there I was immersed in the mass of students. We were all considered to be "debauched," penned up far from the sight of respectable citizens.

Since the excuse of my studies was no longer valid, my determination to live alone and in the city was like a bomb being dropped. All of a sudden, I made myself conspicuous, defied tradition. Became a danger to society and put the family honor in peril.

My father's butcher shop was transformed into a courtroom. Neighbors and acquaintances came to hold counsel. To pronounce their disapproval. I expected it and didn't back down. Lamine supported me. My father's other sons, the ones who had always threatened and fleeced me, raised a hue and cry. Proclaimed that if they'd been listened to, they would have "wiped me out" a long time ago. They wouldn't shed one tear for me. Sharpening his knives, my father swore that he wouldn't let me follow my mother's example.

"You're my daughter. I'm going to have to find you a husband who will break you. And if you rebel, I'll drink your blood!"

And saying this, he aggressively threw a large kitchen knife through the air, planting it in the butcher's block.

However, the greediness of my family quickly got the better of them. In return for a third of my salary, I won their agreement. Accompanied by this warning:

"Watch out! If you dishonor us, we'll kill you. We're keeping an eye on you!"

Nobody tried to impose a husband on me, or even to look for one. That would have meant giving up the allowance that they received each month.

Lamine was in no better shape than I was. His brothers, now

all Islamists, were in league against him, accusing him of being my pimp, a future heretic who would burn in hell . . . The range of infamous terms with which our inquisitors condemn us is great.

"You have entirely prostituted yourselves. Body and beliefs! Bullshit brigades! Terrorist seeds!"

Insults and intimidation were becoming more and more frequent and violent, and Lamine roared:

"Even my father, that pig who swindled people for his own profit, has started doing the same for the FIS. You shouldn't give in to his blackmail. He doesn't have the right to take a penny from you. Come with me, let's split to Algiers!"

"You think they'll leave you alone in Algiers?"

"At least I will have put four hundred kilometers between them and me."

Yacef couldn't, didn't want to, leave his family. I stayed in Oran for him, for my city, for my friends. Lamine "split" all alone. I missed him. Terribly. Yacef and I went to Algiers as often as we could. Lamine came to see me in Oran.

The ease of romantic life inside the confines of campus housing was over with. Back to the interdictions and the intolerance of the city, Yacef and I were forced to hide our love. We defended it in the face of and against everyone. Against my family and his. Against the self-righteous spirit of the neighbors. Against people scandalized by everything.

From then on, to meet me in the evening, Yacef was reduced to comical tricks: park his car as far away as possible from my building. Wait until there was no one at the entrance. Trick the concierge, who, like many others, behaved like a true jail keeper in safekeeping the honor of his fief. At the police's instigation, if he suspected cohabitation or simply a mixed get-together at the place of some singles, he would call the vice squad. At the sight of girls loaded into a van heading for the police station, he smiled ferociously, smoothing his mustache:

Of Dreams and Assassins

"Sluts! Put 'em all in a whorehouse! The country has to be cleaned of this scum!" he spat out at the departing vehicle.

Yacef and I had a code. If he found the entryway lamp out upon arriving at my door, there was danger: one of my father's sons was there for a morality raid. Then Yacef, careful not to put his key into the lock, tiptoed back the way he came in.

Once we were together, we still had to close the shutters, whatever the season. Speak in low voices so as not to arouse suspicion. Before he left, erase the marks of his having been there.

One after the other, our friends got married to escape all of this. Sometimes even before finishing their studies. For ages Yacef's parents had let their son know that it was normal for him to spend time with a loose girl. But one does not marry such a girl.

In spite of these difficulties, living in transgression suited me. Galvanized me. Gave me the feeling that I was triumphing over all stupidity. My need for love grew with the years. Entirely dedicated to its fulfillment, I would hardly have worried about propriety. Would never have thought of marriage, were it not for the country's regression and violence.

Fear seized us. Insidiously. Our life in "sin" could make us targets for any kind of maniac. And there are so many crazy nuts who consider their insanity to be a divine right. So many hoodlums who would have your skin for two cents. So many bloodthirsty people who want to add to their record of murders. We also felt the need to be together. Furthermore, Yacef tolerated less and less the litany of allusions and warnings from his family. One day he decided to face them. Met with an indignant refusal, of course. That their son marry "a slut" was out of the question. "Never!"

No mediation on the part of any friend succeeded in bending them. And, here in Algeria, those men are rare who act without their parents' consent. Especially in the choice of a wife. Armed with patience, we told each other that time was our ally. That the force of our attachment and our desire to live together would make them give in one day. That they would surrender before we would.

Soon our love found refuge in our friends' houses and apartments. The legitimacy of their union protected us. We became true nomads, living sometimes with some, sometimes with others in order not to wear out our welcome.

But our friends quickly had children and less and less space and time for our wanderings. And then we had to tend to the deep depression of my friend Selma, whose lover had just left her.

Yacef was silent and morose. But with the drama ravaging the country, we'd all become like that, wavering between the enthusiasm we felt for life and our fear of death, which struck each day. Between bursts of will and courage and stupor in the face of the destruction. So I attributed his mood to the general atmosphere. How could we escape from the suffocation and terror?

At the end of the academic year, I was promoted to a professorship. Why so soon? I shouldn't have shown so much zeal in the exercise of my functions. Was I the victim of some ill will? In this context, any promotion of a French-speaking person was suspect. Seemed to us to be a blacklisting. Anxious, I went looking for Yacef.

"So you're going to be my boss!"

His clenched face and grating laugh left me no doubt about his feelings. All of a sudden I felt ashamed for both of us. Whereas some of our friends received letters full of insults and threats, or were harassed over the phone, a nomination for promotion froze me with fear and ruffled Yacef. I got hold of myself and told myself that he would have all summer to get used to this idea. And so would I to conquer my fears. That we must resist this psychosis that plunged us into the fear of

Of Dreams and Assassins

everyone and everything. That allowed our own lives to ambush us.

"Why don't you go spend a little time with Lamine? That would change your mood," Yacef suggested to me.

He didn't include himself in the trip. For the first time. Yet we had both been on vacation for a week. I didn't understand him. I needed Lamine's comfort so much. Our complicity. So I decided to go to Algiers. Yacef accompanied me to the airport. When I kissed him, I found his mood so strange that it wrang my heart, and I felt guilty leaving him in such a state.

False Loves

Three days in Algiers. Three days with no news from Yacef. I stare at the phone in vain; it remains silent. I don't understand. Even on the rare occasion when flu kept him at home, he managed to call me at some moment when no censor was nearby. Anguish is gnawing at me. What if something has happened to him? I quickly chase away this thought. Lamine tries to distract me. Without succeeding. Our reunion is spoiled.

"I'm going to call him at his parents' house," decides Lamine, also overtaken by anxiety.

Call him at his parents. My enemies. It's been three days since I've refused to. Lamine knows it. But our patience has run out.

"Yes, please do."

He dials the number. I grab the other receiver. It rings over there in that hostile barracks of a place. No one answers. I call Kamel, a mutual friend:

"I haven't seen him for four or five days. I don't know what he's up to."

We call again in the evening. With no result. I'm tortured by fear. It no longer lets go. I watch the news intently. People killed. As every day. His name is not mentioned. I sigh with relief, but not without a bad conscience. I'm up all night. The following morning I take the plane to Oran. When I get there, I call our friends together, and we all end up at Kamel's, united by the same sense of panic.

"Maybe it's just a dumb problem with the phone. I'm going to go there," Kamel declares.

Kamel returns:

"The house is closed up."

"Have you ever seen that blasted jail open?" I can't help crying out.

"But I rang several times. It's certain there's no one there!" Seeing my grief-stricken look, he adds:

"How stupid I am, I didn't think of asking the neighbors. I'm going to return and knock on their door. They'll certainly be able to give me some information."

While we wait for him, Foued, Selma, Rachid, and I call the police stations and the hospitals one by one. No success.

Seeing Kamel's look upon his return, I scream:

"They've killed him!"

Kamel takes me in his arms and says, his voice breaking:

"He's with his parents in Algiers. He's marrying a cousin."

The news floors me.

I free myself from Kamel's embrace. He stares at me in helplessness. Escape. Escape from myself, from that reality. Suddenly Selma bursts into sobs. It's my turn to laugh. Uncontrollable laughter. That shakes me like a spasm. Selma turns toward me. Slaps me full force. My laughter stops short. I don't feel anything anymore. Just this desire to escape. Selma throws herself into my arms and sobs even more forcefully. I hear myself say to her:

"Don't cry. You know that makes you ugly!"

Where does this calm come from? Selma moves away from me. Through her tears, her eyes show surprise and fear.

"Your face is going to be all puffed up. You know that!"

She turns away and runs toward Kamel's room.

For lack of whiskey, my friends serve themselves wine. Holding glasses in their hands, they look at me with dismay. Hearing the strident child's laughter, they have the look of the people who used to say "she really is crazy." I grab my purse. Kamel leaps toward me.

"Wait! Wait!"

I push him away and rush down the staircase. Outside, the city is gloomy. As usual. The crowd flows by. Flood of people

Of Dreams and Assassins

with the blues. And the same light. The sky's same insolence, a supreme violence.

I walk with my hands stuck in my pockets. Think about Selma, who must still be crying, her wound reopened. Did that wound ever close? No. Tears are never far away in Selma's voice. Even when she's angry. Even when she's joyful or feels mocking. Pain is just behind. Two years ago, having just finished his studies, her lover abandoned her to marry a girl chosen by his parents. Him too. An attitude common to so many students. The elite, *zaa'ma!*

A recluse in her agony, Selma cried for days at my place. The tears, as they infiltrated the skin of her face, would deform it: swollen eyelids, circles under her eyes, pockets under the circles, lips whose shape had been erased . . . Looking at her, I discovered that suffering is also physically ugly.

I would try to reason with her; in vain. She would hear nothing, understand nothing. Just hurt. No longer slept, even with sleeping pills. Would hold her stomach, saying: "It's all empty in there and I'm suffocating. I feel like I have sand in my lungs." Spared herself no pain. Would repeat: "Can you believe it! He was getting ready for that at my side each day." Hunted in her memory for the least hint that should have alerted her to her lover's lies and betrayal. Imagined his parents' joy and the *youyous* of their celebration. Imagined him making love to his wife. Whether she was beautiful or not seemed unimportant to her. But she would get hold of herself: "A doctor, and he leaves me for an ignoramus. How do you expect the attitudes of uneducated people to change toward us?"

She no longer ate. Drank milk and melted away right under our eyes.

"Eat or soon you'll be nothing more than a pile of bones."

"I'm losing weight, for certain. But I'm also becoming bitter. That's even more serious."

She would smoke cigarette upon cigarette to the point of nausea. Until her voice cracked. Sometimes, her body trembled like an addict needing a fix. Sometimes, she began to pace in circles, her movements like those of an autistic. Then, propped

Of Dreams and Assassins

up on a bench, she sank into long fits of exhaustion. When she came out of them, she would ask me: "Is there water now?"

I always watch out for the water to flow. In our life whose blood has been sucked dry, even water has become a rare commodity. I usually leave the bathtub faucet open in order not to miss it. At the first gurgling noises of the pipes, I rush in with containers and bottles. Taken over by a sudden coughing fit, the faucet starts hiccuping and spits out a volley of vile juice. Then the stream becomes continuous and clear.

Having stocked up, I would call Selma. She would quickly slide under the shower and, despite the suffocating heat, completely open the hot water faucet, transforming the bathroom into a steam bath. Her trembling calmed down little by little. She gave me the impression that she wanted to dissolve in the flow of water. Stayed there until the last drop. Until, with a big sucking noise, the pipes sucked their offering back in. She would hardly have dried herself off when shivers and tremors would come over her again. Winter was in her body in the middle of summer.

Later on, deaf to our worries and our warnings to be careful, she began walking all day long around Oran, unable to exhaust her distress.

"You're going to get yourself attacked by the fundamentalists!"

"Aggression is inside me. The most terrible aggression. The kind of aggression that comes from those people you thought were allies. The aggression of enemies would practically be an antidote to it."

Her sleepwalker's look, her robotlike walk, and her wild eyes undoubtedly saved her from the street's violence. She was no longer in Algeria's chaos. She had become that chaos.

She had squeezed her fists so much on the first day that when she returned her palms were bloody. So I cut her nails short. Afterward, I was careful to do it regularly.

When she returned, she would often say: "I don't see people. I don't see places. At times, I no longer even know where I am. I just have the sensation that the streets are torrents washing down human remains. I'm a drop of blood in the torrents."

Her language had also grown poorer. She had closed herself up inside of the obsession, the violence of a few words, a few sentences from which she freed herself only with an explosive voice and stuttering.

I got hold of some more powerful sleeping pills and some whiskey.

"Get drunk and sleep. There's nothing else to do. Time has to pass."

She answered me:

"Time doesn't pass. It's at a standstill."

After several restorative periods of sleep, her still hollow face regained its normal appearance. But even if she stopped crying, a permanent look of agony had taken shape in her eyes. It took her longer to get back normal speech. To recover the depth of her thoughts. To open up to us bit by bit. Yacef, Foued, Rachid, and I tried to distract her. When the boys would leave, the two of us would continue talking until late into the night. Alcohol saved her from despondency, gave her back her anger, her mockery, her force. Happy to see her finally respond, I also got drunk so I could be as close to her as possible. To accompany her in these still fragile bursts that were helping her reconstruct herself.

As soon as she was up, she would start her flight across the city. Sober, she would sink again into her anguish.

To comfort her, I reminded her one evening:

"Look at me—since childhood I've lived in a state of deprivation and absence."

She retorted that I had never felt anything but the melancholy caused by emptiness. As the years passed, this defect had made me absent from those around me. Rejected by the children of the woman who had replaced my mother. And neither woman had any more reality for me. Indifference toward my father. She told me that Yacef's love had saved me, taken me out of this state. That the most frightening abyss is formed only by the loss of happiness. That it exists only in reference to happiness. That the notions of lack and unhappiness and their intensity have meaning and degree only in comparison with fullness. Not in nothingness.

I didn't yet realize how right she was. Her depression frightened me so much that I told myself, "I'll never experience that." It appalled me. She seemed to carry death within her. The death of the Other in her body. Completely internalized. Without the physical reality of death, which could have initiated the work of mourning. She had settled into an endless process of dying.

More than a year later, Selma accepted Foued's love, and they married. Immediately afterward, she announced to me that she was pregnant. The rush with which everything was dealt with disconcerted me. All I saw in it was a gesture of desperation. Alas, the recent sobs confirm my fears. Foued is a good boy. She's lucky to have him. She has recovered her calmness at his side. A certain balance. In any case, she no longer has "an empty stomach." And she'll always have an alibi to cry again. Algeria will see to that.

Before the breakup, where did I get that certainty of being unfit for suffering, at least to such an extent? Breakup—I suddenly understand to what a degree the word suits me. Has always defined me . . . Certainly not with the hope or the will to fall back immediately into my previous disaffection, no. It's that having come out of the latter, I discovered little by little all the facets of feminine dramas here in Algeria. No woman is spared. Not even the best off among us, the students! How many are there whose loved ones have dropped them to go marry virgins subjected to tradition? In university housing, how many melodramas and attempts to commit suicide are there? These crises leave the female students annihilated. Diplomas in hand and the future before them, they feel "finished" because a man has taken their virginity and betrayed them.

From observing the women students, I couldn't then help thinking of the fate of uneducated women. Destitute. Repudiated, thrown onto the street with their children by unscrupulous husbands who keep belongings and apartments. Beaten. Slaves . . . State and society, resistant to progress, remain stubborn in wishing to reduce them to a few miserable functions. To tolerate them only as robots. The tragedy is that currently, they no longer receive any aid or board and lodging, advantages reserved for the weak. Tradition has been broken. With it disappear the few benefits conceded to women. What remains is filth in the minds of people uprooted by rural exodus, disoriented by frustration and confusion. Women, as the fulcrum of this social change, pay the highest price.

Many of those locked up by tradition are now forced to confront the working world in order to feed their children. A world for which they were never prepared. Which was forbidden to them. And in which, once again, they find themselves standing over a mop. Their dignity exposed to the self-satisfaction of an array of bosses. Of the guard of the bosses' boss. The most unlucky women are reduced to begging, to the street.

Heads of state and Western intellectuals sometimes mobilize for oppressed minorities throughout the four corners of our planet. But not for women! Not for the majority that they represent! Not against laws that degrade them. Women are not "the future of men" but represent a shameful silence in a world termed progressive.

Mothers, sisters, daughters, cousins, foreign women, literate or uncultivated, it doesn't matter! It's as if they didn't have a brain with which to understand and inherit the world as full-fledged citizens. No eyes to delight in it or to strike it down. No nose to appreciate its perfumes and to be horrified by its stench. No mouth to kiss, smile, and protest. No palate for feasting. No ears with which to hear everything, even insults strewn in their path. No skin for the caresses that the majority of them never receive. None of that.

It's as if their body and their face were nothing but a sexual organ to be hidden at all cost. In other times they buried them at birth. *Chadors, hidjabs,* scarves, rags of all sorts continue today to shroud them.

Their faces and their hair provoke all sorts of hallucinations. It's as if there's a hell between their legs that threatens to swallow up the universe. Moreover, they have breasts and a depraved uterus that often reproduces its own aberration, another girl.

And the boys, having just barely finished devouring their breasts, are already their censors. They haven't yet spat out their first teeth when they begin to see in women satanic souls. Genetically guilty. And when they finally grow so-called wisdom teeth, their misogyny reaches the height of rage. And to think that it's the illiterate women, the first victims of this education, who inject little boys with the rudiments of the machismo that is going to poison their own lives!

All of this humiliation, topped off by Selma's distress, saturates me. Such that there is no longer any place left in my being for an individual case. Even if it is mine. The scale of collective trauma sweeps away, or at least minimizes, individual fate. Yes, that conviction was already there, well fixed in my head. With neither pretension nor presumption. Just the obvious "I'll never know that," because I had already drunk the dregs of injustice and the affronts inflicted on women. It's more a question of thorough disgust than rebellion. Yes, I was already out of sorts and hung over as a result.

However, I needed this personal disillusionment to better understand the feeling of defeat experienced by other female students. To realize that it undermines what is essential. Those very two emblems of our freedom, knowledge and love. We had those two rights wrenched away. They rehabilitate our entire being. In its dignity. To love is to become strong with two wills so as to confront the intolerance of the masses. To gain knowledge is to intoxicate the spirit with light. And to understand that obscurantism debases all of us. It is to take ownership of one's life. To learn to defend it, to denounce and to say no.

No, we will be neither rejects nor garbage nor inferior pawns of the community.

And what horrible pain when those we have chosen and cherished abandon us for the other side! That of the reactionaries. What's the difference? A luxury, a dead end against the unnameable. So, be they fundamentalists, activists, conservatives, abject, cowardly, or simply fickle, we reject all of them as part of the same hostile caste. At a time when many pay for their differences and their aspirations to another destiny with their lives, this attitude is witness to the profound solitude of women in their fight. And the conditions of their existence are such that the wound will remain perpetually reopened. Forever incurable. Sinful love can only engender and feed false loves. And many among us find ourselves alone with immense unsatisfied dreams of love.

Love, a constellation shining with all of our disillusion.

"If you truly dream, your dream exists, you live it!" Alilou, my only childhood friend, said to me when he took me on board his "sputnik" for a ride through his imaginary planets. Alilou let himself be sucked up by the force of his dreams, as if he had taken off in the face of adulthood betrayals. Fled in the face of independent Algeria's barbarity, which, little by little, darkened men's minds. Men who now kill every day. Kill innocent people. Kill children. Rape and kill adolescent girls and women. Kill intelligence, our differences, our confidence in human beings. Massacre our guests and threaten countries of progress. Lock people into hatred. Dirty the tolerant Islam of this country. Are the AIDS of religion. The assassins of faith.

And in this drama of ashes and blood, the most abominable violence is the destruction of hope. It is the failure of thought that makes the women who succeed in getting an education exiles in their country, as in their society. That's what exile is! For the latter, to cross borders, to put the biggest distance between themselves and their family, between themselves and a country that refuses them freedom is a release.

Algeria has produced so many orphan girls with living parents. So many lone people with numerous siblings, who have lost brothers, sisters, and lovers, at the furthest end of what is forbidden, at the doors of their freedom. For us, freedom was at this price. This has nothing to do with the Western conflict between generations. We have taken a perilous jump across centuries and abysses. And we still keep in us, anchored in us, this sensation of the abyss . . . Some women, torn between the desire to flee and feelings of guilt, commit suicide. Algeria can be proud of one of the highest rates of female suicide in the world!

* * *

I walk up and down the streets with an empty head. For a long time. Then, taken over by furor, I hurry home. Break and tear apart presents from Yacef. Pour out into the middle of the room the drawers containing pictures of eight years spent together. Light them on fire. Poof, a big flame and then nothing. Just a few ashes surrounded by soot and the smoke that darkens the room and makes me cough. I open the glass door that looks out onto a small balcony. Then the front door. The stairwell is empty. At this hour, heat and digestion plunge everyone into a lethargic nap. I pull my mattress all the way onto the balcony. And with a sudden effort, dump it over the railing. I run downstairs. The concierge immediately opens his door halfway. You'd think this guard dog never sleeps. I stop. I take out a bill from my purse and hand it to him:

"I've thrown away a mattress. Could you take care of it please?"

He pockets the bill and follows me outside:

Of Dreams and Assassins

"Hey, American, you throw away a mattress just like that, do you?"

All of a sudden his eyes get big and stare, horrified, at the view of little pale marks like wilted flowers on the mattress. Then, contemptuous:

"Filth! Filth! Go on, get out of here! Get out of here!"

I shrug my shoulders before leaving. After a few steps I turn around. See him dragging the mattress to his place. He doesn't make "filth." Stains are women's sins in detail and in quantity. They say it's written in the Koran. Pleasure is filth? How can the sacred convey such insanity? Filth only piles up in the darkness of certain minds. It fogs their interpretations of the texts. They also pronounce *fatwas* against novelists who disturb them. They also build insult into morality and violence into justice.

The concierge won all the way, money, a mattress, an insult . . . and, he believes, paradise. *Inshallah!*

I glance at my fingernails. They're long. I carefully open my hands. Spread my fingers. Realize, after a second, that my jaws are pressed against one another. So much that my head is being unscrewed. I make an effort to unsolder them. Stare at the people in my path. Lock onto their gaze, their miserable reality, in order not to lose my footing. Tell myself: I'm strong, I'm one of the privileged. Two tears roll down my cheeks. I wipe them angrily. I won't cry! Not for that. Not in this Algeria, where crying, when one is a woman, means giving up. Where tears are no longer any consolation. I'll wait for other times, other countries. For pain that doesn't carry with it so much pestilence and tragedy.

And then what? After love and terror, was it possible for me to avoid despair? Here I am satisfied. Now I'm really alive. A life fulfilled all the way to the heart of woundedness.

After a few days I feel a stinging sensation under my right breast. My skin is red. I consult a doctor.

Of Dreams and Assassins

"You have shingles. It's painful but not serious."

I return with painkillers. Selma greets me with this peremptory declaration:

"The pain you refuse to express is coming out in your skin!"

"Stop bugging her!" interrupts Foued. "It seems there have been a number of cases of shingles recently. A doctor friend was talking to me about it the other day. He said it's linked to anxiety. So you too could have it tomorrow or in a month!"

"Oh, me, I catch everything. Besides, you can catch everything here. We're in the country of contagiousness. The only thing that doesn't seem to take hold is intelligence," Selma ridicules. "The Arabs must have left its genes in Andalusia. Since then, brains rot and only catch the vermin crawling on the southern shore."

When Knowledge Is the First Exile

There, just below us, the sea swells and shines in the moonlight. The rhythmic lapping of the waves licks the rocks. From
the balcony where we've gathered, a stone staircase descends
the cliff and ends in a miniature-sized creek. It's hot. I turn toward Selma:

"A swim after all these crowds! . . . It's stupid to dream of
a swim when the ocean is there, right under my nose."

"It'd be better to dream of it. We'll go swimming tomorrow.
We'd make great targets in this moonlight!"

The threat of the curfew, established in other cities, is use-
less here. Our terror is enough to shut us in. It's absolutely
comical.

"Do you want a little rosé to console you? Foued chilled
some."

"I'd like some."

"And you, Rachid?"

"Yes, please."

Selma gets up and goes inside the house. Her tummy is
quite round now. Five, six months? I no longer know. Sitting
under the lamp, Rachid is reading the newspaper, his back
against the picture window. Stretched out on the floor of the
balcony, hands under his neck, Kamel has dozed off, exhausted
with sadness. This morning we buried his brother, a well-
known doctor, slaughtered by the fundamentalists. We didn't
moan. Didn't cry. We just huddled together and embraced,
our hearts ready to burst.

A meal after the funeral, tea, coffee, and speeches. Everyone was there, neighbors and friends, anger held back, praising the qualities of the deceased.

At the end of the afternoon, Selma, Foued, Rachid, and I came here with Kamel, to the villa of death, on the coast road in Aïn El Turc. My memories and feelings of insecurity made me desert my apartment. I don't set foot there except to pick up some belongings every so often. For a few months now, we've all felt the need to live this way, as a wandering band. Five, six, eight friends, even more. And it doesn't matter what space is available. For now, the overcrowding reassures us. We've once again found our student habits. Except that it's rarely a celebration that brings us together. Fear is an even stronger bond.

The sea is without a ripple. The moon's reflection stretches gently across the water. I need the sea. Its recollection alone was always like a breath of air during my long periods of suffocation in the desert. Contemplating it returns me to the desert. The latter closed me into its vastness. Into its eternity. My eyes became frightened with sublime desolation. The sky's pitiless magnifying glass. Ovenlike days. The light's ecstasy. The dogma of silence. Fear and fascination to the limits of what is tolerable. Dreaming of the ocean freed me from the desert's hypnosis, rolled, carried away my thoughts, rocked my dreaming. Then a light breathing came to me, doubt's swaying, like far-off effusiveness, calls to escape. I'm lost in sea and desert. I melt and confuse them into one image, the shining wound of my freedom.

But this evening, neither the sea's proximity nor the memory of the desert succeeds in calming me. This false calm oppresses me. The odor of the night-blooming jasmine makes me giddy. Everything repels me this evening.

Selma returns with a bottle of rosé and some glasses. Rachid angrily throws down his newspaper.

"What butchery!"

Then, turning toward me:

"Kenza, at the funeral my colleagues just now informed me

Of Dreams and Assassins

that at the end of the academic year, Yacef had asked to be transfered to Annaba."

"Oh yeah?"

"What a bastard! What a coward!" says Selma, indignant.

"Everyone knew that. Except for his pals and you. Nothing works anymore. Whatever is happening to us?"

"From their compassionate looks during the procession, I strongly suspected they knew more than I did."

"It seems his parents built him a beautiful house there but he wanders from bar to bar."

Selma predicts with a ferocious little laugh:

"He'll end up with a few slugs in his cheating brain."

Then, after some thought, she turns toward Rachid:

"Do you think his parents are Fissistes?"

"Frankly, I don't know. How can you tell who's up to what with whom? The bearded ones have shaved. The military are hooded. You don't recognize any longer your brother or your best friend. The state treats us like *laïco-assimilationnistes*. The terrorists want to exterminate us. Torture or murder for the military. Torture and murder for the fundamentalists."

"And he never talked to you about it?"

"He said they were very conservative. But he never . . ."

"Hm, in their case the plunge is sudden. With all the bucks they have, I'm sure they give some to these bands of assassins, even if only to save themselves."

"Money, opportunism, frustration, ignorance . . . they cast their net wide. When I think that even my father began playing pious. It's the height of hypocrisy!"

Rachid interrupts me:

"I don't understand why Yacef acted that way. I would never have believed that he would give in to his parents' pressure one day."

"It's not only that."

"What else?"

" . . . "

"What else? Have you forgotten that here, we don't much like intelligence in a woman? In other places, knowledge is an advantage. Here, applied to women, if it's not depravity, it's at least a nagging suspicion. It really is. That evil is always gnawing at this country. Yacef often said that you were too demanding. The stupidity of machos is reflected in their choices. They prefer idiotic women who directly flatter them. And anyway, by behaving that way, Yacef gains both his parents' blessing and their fortune."

I say to myself, "Wisps of bitterness. Selma is still speaking for herself." I can't keep from recalling Yacef's face when he had cried out: "So you're going to be my boss!"

"What other reason?" insists Rachid.

"Quite simply, no more love perhaps. Or a desire to change partners . . . "

"But he was in love with you!"

"An itch for sex . . . disgustingly trite."

They both look at me as if I had suddenly turned into a demon. That's how it is each time we broach this subject. They would have preferred that I be beaten down and heartbroken. You know, "normal." They would have pampered and consoled me. Pain is so widespread here that with a bit of cynicism one can even admit that the pain of others offers comfort. Diminishes boredom. Conceals our own terror. There is pain for all tastes. For all types of sensitivity: women in the street with masses of children. Without belongings or money. Adolescent girls, cattle to be hacked up after use. Youth without dreams and without hope. Unending bad luck. "Instruction" of which obscurantism is now the only vocation. Tailor-made murders: for the intellectuals, a bullet in the head. Stray bullets for the anonymous and the destitute. A knife to cut the vocal cords of those who speak out. Violence of dogma versus tolerance. Distant murmur that panics and unfurls onto anguish. A backdrop of misery. Allah must have damned the living and the survivors.

Too bad for them. So much the better for me. Moan for months? No. I don't want to. Can't. My pride wounded, I rebelled against and cut off my feelings. The pain of self-mutilation is so violent that it has gotten rid of the earlier

Of Dreams and Assassins

one. I'm left with a stump that I wrap with silence. No gangrene. No depression. Not even bitterness. Just the sensation of a phantom limb. And pretending. By working at it, I end up playing my role perfectly.

Selma and Rachid observe me with curiosity. I feel the need to show off:

"Yacef didn't die. He decided to leave me. I simply dreamed. Then I woke up. You don't feel sad after a dream. You know it wasn't true. But I learned something very important: love is my true dream. Men are interchangeable like any other dream motif. It's Love that I'm in love with. With its light. Too dazzled by its discovery, I didn't see that Yacef carried darkness in him. The blackness of submission. The tenacious mark of machismo."

"You believe you're strong because you don't cry. But there's suffering in everything you say. Your words are worse than your tears!"

I laugh at Selma's pronouncement.

"My words tickle you where you hurt. You know very well that they could come out of your mouth, you who are also capable of wearing the mask of pain."

She gives me a burning look. Rachid interrupts and puts an end to our glaring contest.

"Kamel wants us to stay here until the beginning of the academic year. Even though we're not safer here than we are in the city, at least we have the ocean and pleasant surroundings. And anyway, we can't leave him alone. His brother's murder is a terrible shock."

"The beginning of the academic year? I think you're pretty optimistic with all the threats hanging over us. What we're living now is nothing compared with what's waiting for us."

"What a Cassandra!"

Selma shrugs her shoulders and gives him a cunning smile. I announce to them:

"I think that . . . I think that I'm going to go over."

"Go over?"

Rachid scrutinizes the ocean, turns away:

"To France?"

Of Dreams and Assassins

I nod. He explodes in anger.

"You too? Everything's a shambles! Leave! Run away! Leave the country to the predators!"

"I wouldn't hesitate an instant if I were you," interrupts Selma. "What do you have to lose here? A man who has already abandoned you? Crazy father and brothers who suck your blood and threaten you? The country? The country! What is this country saving for the women? Prosecution for the literate ones, humiliation and suffering for all! During the War of Independence, Algerian women went back and forth in the underground, armed just like their brothers. Now in the underground of brothers, Allah's nonentities lock up adolescent girls for fornication and food. We don't give a damn about a nationalism ignited at our expense."

"It's true. But every cloud has a silver lining. Completely banished from society, women are reacting. Algerian women are magnificent! Look at yourselves, you're magnificent! Much more courageous, tougher than the men."

"Yes, some have liberated themselves. But at what price! And they still have to emancipate their men. They'll have to go at it with a pneumatic drill, because, where women are concerned, our Arabs have hardened neurons. Even those who have completed advanced studies are still caught in a secular glue. The proof is that they need the permission and blessing of papa, mama, and the whole tribe in order to marry. If not, *makayensh!* And on top of that, it's the women who are declared irresponsible and kept under surveillance. We'll have seen everything in this damned country!"

"Thanks for Foued. It's obvious you've married a guy with hardened neurons!"

"I'm not talking about Foued. Him, Kamel, you . . . you're among those few who redeem the male sex. And who reconcile us. There are the ones we marry when the cowardly drop us. And there are those who leave us because we're capable women. Free beings! Because they think that freedom doesn't suit women."

"We're living in a dangerous period, but Algeria is giving a bloody birth to secularism and democracy. And you want to miss that?"

Selma's stinging laughter shuts him up:

"Secularism, democracy, are you nuts or enlightened, my poor Rachid? The schools turn out morons and the population is caught between two terrorisms, that of the army and that of the fundamentalists. The lagging democrats are hidden or in flight. How do you expect . . ."

"But it's just a temporary stage . . ."

I've had enough of these endless discussions that have been going around and around for more than three years. They aren't even discussions anymore. Each one of us has made a shaky building out of his hopes and is trying to rally the others to solidify it. Fragments of reality. Antagonism. Grandiloquence. Vehemence. Bravery. Suspicious whispering . . . everything is mixed together into a veritable cacophony. I intervene:

"Enough! Enough! Let's please talk about something else."

"Talk about something else, she's really good! What d'ya wanna talk about? About plays and films that we haven't seen? About our joie de vivre? About . . ."

"About my departure, for example."

Rachid calms down.

"You haven't been spoiled, that's for certain."

"Lamine was right. My father's dump has become an FIS annex. When I informed him that I won't be giving him any more money, he went into an insane fit. His sons have been on my heels for months. Fortunately, they never know where I hide. The other day, I ran across one of them in the street. The dwarf threatened to tear me to pieces if I didn't go fill the shop's cash register. I can't tolerate any of them any longer. I don't want to tolerate them anymore!"

Rachid taps me on the shoulder:

"I won't condemn you. I know that your life is even more difficult than ours. But what will you do in France? The problem is a job . . . Why don't you go to Tunisia? It must be easier to find a job in Tunisia!"

Of Dreams and Assassins

"I don't know if I'll stay in France. But one thing is for certain: even if it means leaving, I prefer to go where there's no danger of fundamentalism catching up with me. Where no religious mildew will be able to come and pollute my life again."

"Then you'll have to find a desert island!"

A distant look in her eyes, hands around her belly, Selma says:

"France is too close to Algeria. It scares me, too. Anti-semitism is still alive, hatred for immigrants is still used during the least important elections. And now fundamentalism and its *entchadorées* are swarming. All of that tells me there's nothing worth going there for. I want other horizons for my child. Latin America or Australia, for example."

The bouquet of the rosé does us good. We drink together in silence. Silence cuts more and more into our conversations. A closed subject around the inadmissible, fear of the unspeakable. Together we feel torn apart, speak mute monologues. Our words smash into each other without conviction. We are states of solitude condemned to uncertainty.

The din of gulls, like the cries of newborn babies, suddenly tears the silence and startles us. They fly away and hover over the ocean. Their strident cries fade. In the opaline light, their wings shine like crescents that are slowly being shed from the surface of the moon.

"I'll probably try to find a friend of my mother's. Now I want to know. How did she live there? What was she like? How did she die? Did she miss me? I need to reconstruct her in order to find myself a little bit. In order to tolerate the rest."

"You never tried to find out before? How is that possible?"

I don't have the courage to try to explain. To say that before encountering love, I moved toward one single goal: an exam, a diploma. One after another, these helped me to hide what I was missing, to hide my difficulties and the country's growing schizophrenia. To say that the discovery of love plunged me into the vital urgency of quenching my thirsts. To say that after my studies, I wandered with this forbidden love, only finding stability in my work.

As the years passed, I became fed up with the increasingly

pathetic level of the "illiterate bilinguals" starting their university studies, the professional schemers, with the radicalization of misogyny and intolerance, with the fundamentalist attacks . . . This idealized love allowed me to hold on, whereas everything was sinking into violence. But the man that I chose plunged me into mediocrity by behaving like a lout . . . Any attempt to escape from the country's realities or from my own have been obliterated by his behavior. Everything in my head and around me is unsteady. I shrug my shoulders. Selma smiles.

"It's moving!"

I put my hand near hers on her belly.

"Here, here!"

I feel the baby's movements. Selma is suddenly radiant. She swallows a mouthful of rosé.

"Are you going to tell your father and brothers that you're leaving?"

"Only Lamine knows. He says he'll be relieved to see me leave the country. I never tell the others anything! The less they know, the better I do."

"Where do you want to go?"

"To Montpellier. That's where this friend of my mother's lived. And I also have a place to stop off there."

"Why don't you ever talk about your mother's family?"

"Her parents died before she did. It seems that they condemned her behavior. That they tried to make her return to her husband. Without success. I think their fight ended up being final and that they had no further news from her. Afterward, my father arranged it so that I would be cut off from the other members of her family. My mother's detestable reputation facilitated the task. They're no longer in Oran. Since childhood, I've completely lost track of them. But surely they know nothing of her life there."

"And that uncle that your mother had joined in Montpellier?"

"When he was released, he began drinking heavily. And after bearing up under so much mistreatment in prison, he killed himself in a car accident. Alone, against a tree, after a drinking binge."

Of Dreams and Assassins

My plan to leave, which had been forming in my mind since Yacef's disappearance, congealed a while ago, in the crowd at the funeral. Sick of seeing the best of us transformed into stiff corpses. Sick of tombs. Sick of rapes, bloody stories, and other reports of nightmares in our newspapers, on our radios. In the streets. Sick of threats and family shackles. Sick of the different faces of abjectness. Sick of living in suspense, between fear and precariousness, with no future. All of that is way too heavy for my little self. Go far away. I don't yet know where. But after a period in Montpellier. I first have to go in search of this woman, my mother's friend. I have to know. Nothing more, just understand that first abandonment.

Their discomfort bothers me. Foued comes and joins us. He sits next to his wife and puts his arms around her. I try to change the subject.

"What were you doing?"

"I watched a movie on Channel 2. Fortunately, we have some fresh air from the French TV stations."

Rachid begins talking about some program. I take advantage of this distraction and get up:

"Good night. I'm going to bed. The day's trials have wiped me out."

"Stay a little longer. It's not late."

"You don't want another glass of rosé?"

"No, no thank you."

I leave them and return to my room so as to cut short any other questions.

I can't wash. We arrived in Aïn El Turc too late to stock up on water. We only have three or four bottles of Saïda mineral water to drink. And we're afraid to take advantage of the sea washing at our feet. I pick up a book before going to bed.

Pavese's *Le bel été* doesn't manage to capture my interest. Death haunts my mind. The death of academic friends, of women, of the young, of poor people . . . The death of Abdel Kader Alloula, famous son of Oran and of the Algerian the-

Of Dreams and Assassins

ater, death of the anonymous . . . Electric shock after electric shock, uninterrupted, I feel annihilated. I see my family members. Expressions full of mute cries. Faces lined by anxiety. I see other faces molded by frustration and barbarity. I want to flee. Flee far away. In vain I repeat to myself: *barka, barka!* Nothing calms me. The tension and the fever that surround me make my laughter grating. Exasperation is an integral part of body and mind.

A few days ago, Selma received a letter with awkward writing on the envelope.

"What's that?"

She looked at the postmark.

"It was sent from here."

"Open it and see."

I watched her open it with apprehension. She became as white as the piece of cloth that she pulled out with two fingers. She turned the envelope upside down. A little piece of soap fell into the palm of her other hand. She looked at me with eyes dilated by fear and amazement.

"You know what that means?"

It wasn't a question but a cry of horror in the face of the monstrosity of this anonymous and silent threat. Just that, two elements of the funeral ceremony, soap and a shroud.

"Don't worry. It must be an asshole from your neighborhood who's amusing himself at your expense."

"Amusing himself at my expense? With that? Who can have that much of a grudge against me?"

If only I knew! If only I could be sure that it was just a grim joke.

The same day—was it coincidence?—downstairs, a child yelled from behind me:

"Hey, *la Francis,* you'll see, the mujahideen will kill you too."

I turned around. There were five or six little boys killing themselves laughing. And staring at me insolently, one of them slid his index finger across his neck, meaning that I would have my throat slit.

"From one ear to the other!" added one of his friends.

The others laughed even harder. The laughter of angels. The words of monsters. As if "whores! whores!" forever thrown in our faces would result only in threats. A people that has such disdain for its feminine half, that trains its children for misogyny and fanaticism, in the same way one trains a dog, is working toward its own misfortune. Thirty years of preparation for ugliness. And now, the inquisition and hell.

I tried to laugh about it. For quite a while, fear has been like a spider weaving its web around us. And death spreads its stench everywhere, even in the mouths of children whose eyes are angelic. Who will tell me if there are still any Alilous among this country's little boys? How I would like to believe so!

Somebody knocks at the door of the room I'm occupying.

"Come in!"

Kamel's head appears in the opening:

"May I?"

"Yes, yes. Did they wake you up with their endless talk?"

"It's more the hardness of the floor that woke me up. I had pins and needles in my arms and legs. Did I sleep for long?"

"Two solid hours."

He closes the door, comes toward me, sits at the foot of the bed. I prop my elbows up on the pillows.

"This is my nephew's room."

"Yes, I know."

He speaks for himself. Lets out a sigh. Closes his eyes and forces back his tears. Continues:

"He spent June and July here with his parents. Here he is an orphan in mid-August."

Kamel was very close to his brother and felt great admiration for him. The vice tightens a notch in my chest. I don't know what to say to him, not a word of consolation.

He moves the bed lamp to light up my face. Stretches his legs out onto the floor. Puts his head back onto the edge of the bed. Looks at me and says:

"Apparently, you want to go to France."

Of Dreams and Assassins

Kamel's girlfriend left him for a big shot in the city. His dark curls crown his face. Offer a beautiful contrast to his hazel eyes. His distressed look pains me. The similarity of our situations has woven a close feeling of fraternity between us. I realize I'm going to miss him terribly.

"Yes."

"Doesn't that hurt you?"

"In any case, I'll be less stressed there than I am here. I won't feel hunted by the beasts in our housing projects anymore."

"Hm . . . that must be a different kind of anxiety. I don't know if it'll be less powerful. It's hard to abandon everything with a feeling of powerlessness and defeat!"

"I don't know what I'll do. I want to leave. Leave so as not to slide into insanity."

"You'll have to get a visa. That's more and more difficult."

"I'm going to telephone Barbara Combes. She'll send me a letter proving that I have a place to lodge. And then I'll file for a leave of absence at the rectorate. I'll manage, but I will leave. You know Barbara. She came to see me several times."

"Yes, yes. She was your French professor, right?"

"All through secondary school. In fact, she was more than that. During my adolescence, she was the only adult in whom I confided. Her presence and her understanding helped me a lot. We never lost contact. For a long time she's had an apartment on the beach near Montpellier. Since she knew I was born in that city and that my mother lived there, Barbara has often invited me to join her there during vacation or to stay there alone. She lives in Paris. You know, I feel torn between the desire to know who my mother was and the fear of what I could discover. It's completely absurd. As if the irreparable were not already confirmed!"

"No, no, I understand that . . . After all, what's happening to us is crazy. You lose sight of friends. You ask for news of them. People tell you: they're in France, in Tunisia, or in Morocco. And the last straw is that you're relieved they're not dead! Not them. But on that scale, it becomes dramatic."

" . . . "

"We're going to miss you."

"I'll think of you. I'll call you. Will I be able to leave my car in the garage here? I saw that there's room. Outside, I'd be too afraid that it would be used by the Islamists or disappear for spare parts."

"Yes, no problem. Be careful of Frenchmen. They're always on the make!"

I can't manage a smile. Neither does he. We look at each other without knowing what to say. I end up asking:

"Can you please bring me a glass of rosé?"

He gets up and leaves. I admire his lanky body and say to myself: I should have loved him. He's on my side. Our failures have reinforced our friendship. Our hearts are still ravaged.

I tuck my head into the pillow. Close my eyes. Pretend to sleep. Kamel returns and must be looking at me. A long moment passes by. Then I hear him sigh. His breath brushes against my face. I imagine him bent over me. He places a kiss on my forehead. Turns out the light and creeps out quietly. In the darkness I smile. True happiness, this chaste kiss.

My friends' muffled voices reach me. Every night it's like this. Sometimes there are bursts of laughter. Then discussions interrupted by silence. Never-ending. They don't rebuild the world anymore. They search the ruins, sometimes angrily, sometimes powerless or concerned. The collapse is so great. Thirty years of lies about our identity. Thirty years of falsification of our history and mutilation of our languages have killed our dreams, made us exiles in our own country.

Montpellier

I let myself relax with the rocking motion of the train. At my window, the same sky as in Oran. The same September light. This light that tumbles down onto shapes. Elongates the shadows. Plays with the contrasts. Its depth of field and the nuances of its colors sculpt and reinvent nature each instant. In Oran, I no longer paid any attention to the play of light. The blue color of the sky became nothing more for me than the condensation of the earth's violence. Even our most simple desires were crushed. Towns pass before my eyes. Arles, Tarascon, Nîmes . . . A concentration of apartment buildings right next to stone houses. A lattice of tile roofs surrounding the urban centers. Small gardens whose composition often looks to me like a model of meticulousness. The same countryside as on the other side. Greener. Bushy and rocky hills. A mosaic of thickets, scrublands, fields, and vines, dotted with cypress. Everything goes by so quickly. Two words bang around in my head to the rhythm of the train: clean and prosperous.

The Montpellier train station. The foreign city where I was born. Where my mother died. A place, a connection between my birth and her death. Also, the point of rupture of our two lives.

The train stops. I hurry to get off. My heart is beating hard enough to burst. In the commotion, I feel like I'm floating. I abandon my belongings at the checkroom. Walking revives my legs.

An attractive elderly woman smiles at me in the street. I see in the smile a sign of welcome. Say to myself that I'm taking my desires for realities. How can I ignore that I'm one of the undesirables here? I've read and I've heard speeches reached by consensus against those from the South. Threshold of tolerance. The right and the left's charters. Repeated police excesses whose victims, what luck, are always Maghrebian! National Front and all the rest of it. With the satellite dishes, Algiers and Oran vibrate to the echoes of Paris. Paris has fun scaring itself by bringing up Algeria. Solidarity and rejection, Manichaeism, resentments, and so many bogeymen on both sides.

The street that I took leads to a big square. An operatic decor extends a theater. The cosmopolitan flow of people goes by between the clients seated in the sun at the Grand Café Riche and those seated in the shade of Les Trois Grâces. There's plenty of marble if you want it. Sprays of water murmur in fountains the size of temples. I repress my laughter at the idea of the damage that a horde of kids turning up from home would cause here. Spit spattered like grasshoppers all over this marble. Shop windows and frescoes handed over to the "wall holders" like across the sea. Here I am giving in to clichés! But clichés have one thing that is frightening: they're often founded on a base of truth. Generalizations and stupidity weave the rest.

My eyes look for a sign; "PLACE DE LA COMÉDIE" shows me what I'm looking for at the corner of a wall. I find this comedy superbly human. A paradise when one comes from a country of tragedies.

I go in search of the old city. Open squares without the crowds you'd find back home. Streets without the flood of youth. Many gray-haired heads. Little despair at the foot of the walls. Walls without cracks. Dog shit instead of spit wads on the pavement. Every consistency and size. No crowds around the churches. Faith behind closed doors here. In a street closed to vehicles, I stop and stare at a Maghrebian woman. Old-fashioned dress. Henna on her feet. Gilded slippers. A scarf wrapped around her head. And on every inch of her uncovered skin, the havoc of tattoos. No doubt she has just arrived. After so many years spent in France, Zana Baki certainly doesn't stroll around dressed that way.

"What's the matter, my daughter?" the woman inquires gently when she sees my astonished look.

I get a grip on myself. Answer the first thing that comes to mind:

"Do you know by chance Zana Baki from Oran?"

"Zana Baki? Where does she live?"

The woman doesn't hide her surprise. A lie saves me from ridicule:

"It's funny how much you resemble her!"

"That happens," the tattooed woman answers philosophically.

"Excuse me."

"That's all right, my daughter, salaam."

"Salaam."

Furious with myself, I leave. After all, I'm not going to melt in front of each Maghrebian woman. "Do you know Zana Baki from Oran?" How stupid! How many immigrants are there in this city? Where do they live? They're certainly parked somewhere, aren't they? First thing to do, then: buy a map of the city and a guide.

I reason with myself in vain. Sure enough, each time I see a Maghrebian woman from a distance, my legs tremble. And if I stay silent until reaching her, my eyes interrogate her, scrutinize her shamelessly. I must say that they flabbergast me. To strut about like that in the streets of France, with their flashy clothes and their little guilty look of women who have simply forgotten their veil at home, floors me it's so unusual.

It takes me some time to understand the true nature of my troubled feelings, the explanation for this pity tainted with derision that seizes me when I see them. For now, the search for Zana Baki is only an illusion. It's just that in each one of them, I have the strange feeling that I'm encountering my mother's ghost. As if a wandering ghost, multiple copies of

Of Dreams and Assassins

my mother, were always there. As if she were unfolding different shapes of absence for my arrival. Different sketches of a body in exile. I end up admitting that to myself, and my heart contracts. I remain perplexed. Where does this sensation come from? From the lost expressions of these women? From their looks, glued to the base of the shop windows in order not to confront those of the natives? From their strange appearance of being veiled women without veils? Of being enslaved women in the midst of liberty? From their separation from the modern norms of this country? Or does it come from me? From this word "mother," which, for lack of memories, lacks substance? From my projection of the word onto unknown women who live on this earth? I can't clarify this puzzle. Regretfully put it out of my thoughts.

I find the post office. Barbara's package is there in my name, general delivery. She has put labels on the keys. Front door. Garage. Car. A pretty swimming suit, a pareo, perfume. There's also a letter that I read quickly. I'm lucky to have Barbara.

I continue my walk in the "historic center" of town. It's so small that every three strides I find myself again at the Place de la Comédie. Fascinated by the maze of streets, I immediately turn around. Admire the building entrances, the interior courtyards glimpsed through the opening of a door. The fountain basins and the vases decorating them. Eaten away by lichen. Bathed in pink shadow. The patios, the stairs, diagonal casement windows, the subtle range of colors of the stone, the craftsmanship of the wrought iron, the workmanship of the gates . . . If the squares remind me of theaters, the tiny streets seem like museum galleries. They tell the story of centuries of sedentary life. The ancient shelters and protects the modern. The products of a consumer society are displayed like works of art. Cases of shop windows. Sometimes on antique columns. My eyes don't know what to look at. So many things that I had never seen except on TV. The feverishness of the discov-

Of Dreams and Assassins

ery, the overabundance and luxury, end up making me dizzy. I close my eyes. Suddenly remember that I haven't eaten a thing since breakfast. It's past three o'clock. I go back toward the Place de la Comédie. I choose Les Trois Grâces. The Grand Café Riche reminds me too much of the café of the same name in Oran where *zazous* harass passing girls. And then it also seems to me a little too . . . snobbish.

I order a ham sandwich and a beer. One of my dreams is coming true. A dream that was never fulfilled in Oran. Simply this: alone in a café, having something to eat while drinking a beer. Without being refused. Without insults. Without brutality of any type. An everyday matter here, of course. What happiness for me! I'd like everyone to be aware of it. But how could these people around me suspect that I am living an exceptional moment? They don't know. Can't know. All I notice is a pleasant glow in the eyes of one or two men. Nothing insistent. There are so many other young women sitting there.

I smile, enjoy, and closely watch the neighboring tables, the passersby. When I've finished my lunch, I have a cigarette. Less out of desire than to measure the entire extent of my liberty. To smoke outside! I smoke and am carried away all alone. Smoke and blow my smoke to the sky. Smoke and smile. Smoke and almost choke myself. I'm being foolish, right? With my self-satisfied look, I feel suddenly like a cigarette ad for Les Trois Grâces, for France. I burst out laughing and put out my cigarette. Down there, liberty was a battle each second. Dissidence and vehemence. And the de-effervescence of pleasure on a regular basis. I didn't suspect that here I was going to first appreciate it through small, relieving gestures. Taboos that give way. I didn't know that liberty would for me be physical lightness before becoming real in my mind. I'm going to have to get used to this feeling of weightlessness. For to no longer feel on oneself the vermin of the multitudes of masculine stares and the extreme tension of Algerian streets causes me such dizziness. I am moved and drunken because of this deliverance. I realize that. A wave of joy invades me and then culminates in pain. My view is fogged up. Two tears roll down my cheeks, which burn with shame. Here I am giving in to sentimentality and making a show of myself!

From a neighboring table, a man leans toward me.

"What's the matter, miss? Can I help you?"

I scrutinize him. Hair the color of mature wheat, steel eyes, a nice frame.

"No, no, it's nothing. I'm crying from joy."

I lower my eyes to hide my embarrassment. He hesitates a moment and then lifts his glass.

"Well, may it last! But without tears!"

I lift my glass too:

"To your health!"

The pleasure of the moment sharpens in me the feeling of waste. My joy cannot be complete. It has a dark side. In one gulp I drink the rest of my beer and get up. The man observes me. His eyes staring at me make me suddenly nervous. My whole body suddenly contracts, and I feel the same exasperation as across the sea. Disappointment and resentment would spoil my day if he were to decide to follow me the way Algerians do. I leave the place. Move away. Turn around. The man is sitting in the same place. He looks at me. I want to smile at him with gratitude. My mouth doesn't obey. My jaws clench. I turn away to hide a grimace. Hurry toward the train station. Pick up my bags and take a taxi to the sea. I have decided to allow myself this luxury.

The taxi driver looks at me inquisitively before starting the car.

"Palavas-les-Flots, please."

"Okay, Pue-la-vase!"

"Why Pue-la-vase?"

"Because of the ponds and the *malaygue* . . . you didn't know that?"

"I'm not familiar with Palavas."

"Are you Brazilian?"

"No, no."

"In any case, Latin American."

Of Dreams and Assassins

"Not at all. I'm Mediterranean."

Hey, it's the first time I've said that. Where does this sudden urge to belong to such a vast community come from? Before, I just called myself Oranian, that's all. Oranian with pride and a bit of arrogance. Is it from straddling the Mediterranean? Is it because I need to include myself in a geographic grouping extending beyond the framework of Algeria, now that the development of fascism in the country throws people like me out? Am I Mediterranean only out of opportunism? Or is it because, despite the unusual luxury and anonymity dazzling me, I don't manage to feel entirely foreign here? For the moment I can't answer that. My thoughts are troubled.

"Moroccan?"

"No."

The chauffeur's laughing eyes sparkle in the rearview mirror. He's quite taken with his guessing game.

"Tunisian?"

"No. Why did you skip Algeria?"

"I don't know. Things are going badly down there. So you're Algerian?"

"Yes. What's *malaygue*?"

"In the summer an algae grows on the surface of the ponds and smothers them. They begin smelling like rotten eggs. It's very unpleasant. Say, where you come from they don't like women very much."

I don't answer. No desire to talk about that now. Need silence. Inveterate chatterboxes, these taxi drivers, wherever they're from.

After an inquisitive glance in the rearview mirror, the man's face clouds over and his attention returns to the road. He understands.

"Turn the meter back on. It's in the cupboard to the left of the front door," Barbara says to me in her letter. I push the switch. Pots rattle as the refrigerator starts up somewhere in the back. I turn on the lights and close the door behind me.

Of Dreams and Assassins

Go farther into the apartment. A bedroom and a living room look out over the sea. A room in the back opens out onto the ponds. The kitchen is separated from the dining room only by a bar. A big table stands in the center of the room. One of the walls is covered with books. Guard against boredom!

I go from the window looking out onto the pond to the balcony with the sea view. On one side, flamingos sit on the surface like big water lilies. On the other, a few swimmers are stretched out on the beach; in the distance, a white sail. Everything here emanates the peace that spreads over the water.

I fill the ice trays before going shopping. Leave my bags where they are, in the middle of the living room.

"The Méhari should start without any problem. It's only been sitting for twenty days," Barbara's letter tells me further. I open the garage. The car starts on the first try. I'm a bit apprehensive about driving here. But the street is deserted, and the pleasant sensation of being at the wheel of a convertible quickly takes away my worry.

Used to the empty store shelves and to the "shackles" of waiting for a possible delivery of oil, tomato paste, soap, or whatever other basic foodstuffs, over there, I'm floored by the displays here. Spend a good hour admiring everything: fresh produce, frozen foods, whole, cut, mixed, vacuum packed, in cans, jars, tubes. A huge variety of sauces, cookies, sweets, jams, drinks . . . This is just a small temple of consumption. What about the giant ones? One day I'll go visit one of them.

I have to force myself not to go on a spending spree. I changed all my savings on the black market. Fourteen dinars for one franc. Here I'm going to have to economize more than I did in Algeria. The savings imposed by shortages in Algeria are a real challenge here. And I must keep enough money as I head toward a still uncertain future.

Back in the apartment, I put away my purchases. Grab the bathing suit and the pareo that Barbara sent me. Six o'clock. On the beach, a handful of people. The water is colder than in Oran. The air too. That's fine by me.

I doze off. When I awake, the sun is down. The beach is

empty. It's certainly the first time that I've felt secure enough to give in to a nap, alone, on a beach. I have the feeling I've slipped into someone else's life. A free life that is dragging my own along like a ball and chain. For in my heart, joy and anguish are still at war with each other. How can I liberate myself from that?

After a shower, I leave the pastis that I bought and serve myself a whiskey from Barbara's bar. The burning sensation does me good. Standing on the balcony, I watch the sea. Imagine my friends sitting on the terrace over there, across the way. At this hour the night-blooming jasmine is beginning to perfume the coast-road air. The odor of wet earth is also apparent when, after the afternoon heat, the gardens finally get some water. And the aroma of basil, coriander, and cinnamon at the kitchen windows. But over there, the sunset is no longer an invitation to stroll on the beach and the seafronts. Over there, the colors of twilight are no longer either an appeasement or an inspiration to dream; rather, they are the cosmic image of the blood of victims. This undecided hour is sadness suspended, like our lives, between two violences. And above the terror of the people, the muezzin's voice resounds like a call to death.

Are Selma, Foued, Rachid, and Kamel sipping a glass of rosé in order to drown their boredom? I lift my glass to their memory. And after looking briefly at the telephone, resist the desire to call them. I'll do that later. I have to learn again what solitude is. Solitude in a state of freedom. Will liberty be more merciful to me here?

As I try in vain to taste each pleasure of my first hours here, I can't help being down there at the same time.

With a bit of charcuterie, a salad, and some cheese, I'll have a feast. The refrigerator is now full of products unavailable or sold at exorbitant prices at home. But I must go out to set myself free from the fear that the approach of darkness arouses in me. From the obsessiveness that makes me check, every five minutes, that the front door is really locked. From all the incoherence, the absurdities, and the inhibitions created by

Of Dreams and Assassins

fear. I want to discover nightlife in a small seaside resort without terrorism and without prohibitions.

The ringing of the telephone startles me. I eye it distrustfully. Remember I'm in France. Finally pick it up.

"Hello, Kenza, it's Barbara. Did you have a good trip? Is everything okay?"

"I'm fine, and you?"

"Fine, fine. Is the apartment okay?"

"Great! I can tell I'm going to have a good time here. Thanks for everything, Barbara."

"Were you able to change enough money?"

"Yes, yes, no problem. Are you kidding! It's a very advantageous trade for expatriates."

"Good. Listen, honey, you have to contact the people from the Comité de Défense des Intellectuels Algériens. They may be able to help you stay here. Don't return, Kenza. I'd be too frightened for you."

"Intellectuals? You're joking. Who's interested in the millions of women and young oppressed and destitute over there? The ones who have been suffering forever! Barbara, a whole population is in danger! In spite of today's threats, I'm one of the lucky ones! The proof is that I'm already protected even if I don't yet know what will happen in the days ahead."

"It won't be easy. But for the moment exile is better than death over there. Dead, you won't be able to do anything more, for yourself or the others."

"I don't know if I'll want to stay here. First I'm going to spend a week relaxing. I really need to. After, I'll try to find this friend of my mother's."

"Okay, then come to Paris. I'll help you with the necessary steps. Please don't return to Algeria!"

"Maybe. I want to get some information about the countries where I can get my university degrees recognized. I think I need to go very far away. I'll have to have a complete change of scene in order to forget. You know, just a little while ago, I fell asleep on the beach. I dreamed I was walking in a snow desert. I woke up with an extraordinary feeling of peace. It's

Of Dreams and Assassins

not the first time this idea has crossed my mind. To walk in a white desert. To have completely different people around me."

"We'll talk about all that. I'll come down and see you after some time."

"If you want, but don't worry about me. Everything will be fine."

"Try to have fun. A big hug! I'll see you soon."

Barbara. Through the years, the professor has become a friend. A tenderness that has never failed me, never betrayed me. Ephemeral or profound, dazzling or slow to achieve, mirage or miracle, any love, any affection is amazing. Only the test of time separates the wheat from the chaff.

Slim the Glider

There's a crowd along the canal in Palavas. In the store windows, summer clothes on sale and all sorts of cheap junk to attract the strollers. The restaurant prices are too high for my wallet. I resort to a pizzeria.

"What a crowd!" I say to the waiter.

"They're just the neighborhood people. The season is over. The vacationers have left. The children have gone back to school. But since we often have Indian summers, people come here to breathe, to make vacation last longer."

"To make vacation last longer." Down there, people kill time and time kills, each day. Down there, misery, boredom, and violence make a fabulous coast a disaster area.

The aperitif stroll comes to an end. There are fewer and fewer passersby. The pirouettes of an adolescent on a skateboard attract my attention. He's dark. Fifteen or sixteen years old. He takes off, jumps, twirls around, abruptly halts at the edge of the quay. My breath stops: he's going to fall into the canal or break his neck on one of those small boats! He takes off again like a bolt of lightning. Disappears from view. Comes back alternating between acrobatic jumps and dizzying stops. I'm the one who's dizzy. I have the feeling that I'm hallucinating. This adolescent weaving his way through the people strolling. His cap of hair, his complexion the color of August dates. He comes to me from my childhood and from the desert. He's hardly five or six years older, whereas I've taken on twenty-three years, doubled by the Algerian disaster. I control myself from crying out: Alilou!

Of Dreams and Assassins

The boy must have noticed my interest, because he lingers at the pizzeria where I'm seated. I'm no longer afraid for him. I'm too moved. He dazzles me. I even let myself go so far as to applaud, as I applauded Alilou's exploits. He smiles at me and offers me a veritable ballet. The few passersby stop. Form a circle around his acts of prowess. After a second, turning his back to his admirers, the boy whizzes down the sidewalk. Comes toward me. And with a clatter of wheels stops in front of my table.

"Good evening, could I bum a smoke, please?"

"Yes, here, help yourself. It's not very good for your health."

"And for yours?"

I smile without answering.

"Never mind! Where're you from?"

"From Algeria, and you?"

"Me, I'm half Malian, half Algerian, and half French."

"Gosh, only three halves! In any case, you're a pro on your skateboard."

He puts on false modesty.

"What do your parents do?"

"My mother does housework. I don't know my father. He returned to his village before I was born. He never came back."

Seeing my sympathetic look, he adds with forthright mischievousness:

"Don't sweat it. I was born with that. I don't know what it is to have a father. So I don't miss it. Besides, I'd have preferred simply being a bastard."

"Really?"

"Yeah! No kidding, it's better to be a bastard. You don't know who your dad is. He's at the other end of the world not giving a damn about your mug. He doesn't exist! He didn't take anything! Nothing! And you don't even have his name. So you're free. No worries!"

"I don't think you can be freer or more peaceful by being unaware of whose child you are. No more than if you know your parents are degenerates or not around."

"What a calamity! Thank you for the degenerates. I still prefer the ones who aren't there."

Of Dreams and Assassins

We laugh together.

"And you know what else? For me my mother is everything all rolled up in one. My mom's great."

"A lot of them are like that over there. By dint of having to face all sorts of distress . . . it's a question of survival. It's that or let yourself die."

"You're full of hate."

"Too bad I'm not."

"Too bad? You see! You talk like someone lugging around a bundle of hatred. I don't give a damn about other women. I'm talking to you about my mother. MY MOTHER IS UNIQUE. Are you a femi-ma-jig or something?"

"Femi-ma-jig? Feminist?"

"Yeah, a little or a lot?"

"I'm talking to you about survival. You answer femi-ma-jig. I don't think we're on the same wavelength."

"But you were born here!"

"No."

"How long have you been here?"

"Since this morning."

"You should have said so! Now I'm tuning in to you one hundred percent. It's normal to have hatred when you're a woman from the other side."

"They don't have 'hatred.' They're missing love, recognition, liberty, justice. Some are full of rage, others are fed up. Others have been so humiliated that their sensitivity has festered and they've been muzzled. So you see, hatred . . . "

"You talk in images, like my mother."

"Our speech is full of metaphors. I know that in France people don't like that very much. And I don't give a damn!"

"Don't go into a huff; it was just a comment."

"Yes, but it's a criticism from other mouths. Whereas we are ourselves a metaphor of French. Purified Parisian French can't touch us or work for us unless it's chiseled with our images. With their flashy colors and their excesses. It's a question of distance and temperature. Of appropriation, too."

The youth observes me with a sly little look. Puffs haughtily on his cigarette:

"Thanks for the lessons, madame."

His board begins sliding again and moves away from me. Lessons! I didn't come here to give lessons to the French, even if they are dark! Shit, even here, I can't say two words without pouring all of the Algerian mess into people's faces. I've unwittingly made this boy run away.

"Wait, wait!"

He stops.

"I'm sorry for having clobbered you with 'lessons.'"

"You didn't clobber me. What you said interests me."

"Can I offer you something to drink?"

The board makes a big circle and slowly brings him back to me.

"If you want."

He said that with his lower lip full of self-importance. He slowly settles in front of me. Monsieur deigns to accord me this favor. And how! But as soon as he's sat down, his eyes sparkle again with mischief. They hold the same fascination for me as did Alilou's: two black lights that make the opalescent center shimmer. Their brilliance comes from this contrast. Curled eyelashes create moving shadows on his cheek and accentuate the depth and magic of his look.

He is attentively working to balance a long column of ashes at the tip of his cigarette, which he tries to hold up straight. I hold out the ashtray.

"I don't smoke for real. It was just an excuse to talk to you."

"For real," like Alilou says. Do big dreamers, acrobats need to punctuate their sentences with these words so as not to fly away and cut themselves off completely from reality? This expression intensifies my emotion. The adolescent thinks he has once again floored me. Starts laughing. I laugh too in order to shake myself. To emerge from the past. The waiter arrives. Serves him his Coca-Cola.

"What's your name?"

"Slim, and you?"

"Kenza."

"That's an old-fashioned name."

"Yes."

Of Dreams and Assassins

"So you took off, too. Frankly, that's the only thing left to do, especially if you're a girl! Yuck, the guys down there went crazy. The FLN made the *hittistes*. The Fissistes made them crazy."

"That is to say?"

"That is to say walking catastrophes. Kamikazes of unhappiness. They'd do anything to blow up their own mug. It's sad!"

"Do you know Algeria?"

"I only know it through my mother and the people from down there. I don't want to go there."

"Why?"

"Algerians are snobs to dark people like me. My mother's parents got angry with her when she married a black. And when my father abandoned her, they said it was to be expected from a black. That she got what she deserved. They didn't even want to see her anymore."

"She hasn't seen them again?"

"Oh, yeah! A long time ago. Are you kidding, they very quickly learned they could take advantage of her."

"How?"

"Each time, the whole Algerian *smala* falls on top of us and puts us in the poorhouse. As if my mother were loaded. They don't give a damn that she slaves away all year long. They leave with suitcases and bags full of presents for all the grandchildren, the aunts, the uncles, the cousins, the friends . . . And afterward we tighten our belts. It's absolutely disgusting! Especially since they've never really forgiven my mother. They whisper about being 'dishonored' and they make twisted allusions! It makes me puke. I tell my mother: 'They're blackmailing you, and you, you don't walk, you run straight for it!' She answers me: 'Drop it my son, Allah is great.' In the meantime it's not Allah who fills her pockets. My mother is too good."

After a glance at his watch:

"Shit, I've got to scram if I don't want to worry her. I have to return on foot."

"Return where?"

Of Dreams and Assassins

"To Montpellier."

"Why on foot?"

"My bike ran out of gas a little while ago. On the way into Palavas."

"So, you can refill the gas."

"Thanks for the information. I don't have any more cash."

"I can lend you some if you like."

"Are you trying to pick me up or what?"

At my offended look, he adds in a debonair manner: "Don't get mad. I'm kidding. And anyway I'm the one who went after you."

"Oh yeah?"

"Yeah. I wasn't buzzing around here like a bee for nothing. I was attracted to you. But I wasn't on the make just for the fun of it. Anyway, you're too old for me."

"Hm, you're diplomatic!"

"Well, isn't it true? I don't put on airs with words. I get to the point. I don't bother with images . . ."

A little half-smile. I don't react to the hint.

"Do you often do that?"

"Sometimes . . . and even with grandmothers, grandfathers, fathers. People that I like yakking with."

"And are you attracted to these people?"

"Yeah, my sense is rarely mistaken."

"And why do I interest you, besides being a girl alone at night?"

"You come from over there with your big hatred and you don't know what to do with it. I didn't know that yet. But I saw your lost look."

"You're as good with your nose as you are with your skate-board."

"Nobody's ever said that to me . . . But you know, about the money, I never accept it from anyone. Except from my mother."

"So I'll take you back by car."

"And my bike? I can't leave it."

"We'll take it too. I have a Méhari."

"Great, then! That's really nice of you!"

Of Dreams and Assassins

Then suddenly he says, taken aback:

"You arrive today and you already have a car?!"

"It's not mine. Someone's lending it to me."

"Just the same, so you're not that lost . . . my sensor must be off today."

"Undoubtedly."

"So much the better for you. Shall we go?"

I pay my bill and we leave.

"This morning I filled the tank. Afterward a friend borrowed my bike. 'Just to take the errand basket to my mother,' so he said. This evening I was in such a hurry to get here. I didn't see he'd emptied the tank."

"Why were you in a hurry?"

"To stroll around the boats, you know! When it grabs me, it makes me crazy. I charge down here really fast."

"You like them that much?"

"I'd die for one! When I'm older I'll have one. I don't know how yet. But I'll have one. On my word as a crazy!"

"Have you already done some boating?"

"Yeah. Sometimes I go with a friend. His father has a beautiful boat. Sometimes at summer camp, too. The rest of the time, I'm satisfied with looking at them and skating across the asphalt."

"You're really great on your skateboard."

"I have roller blades, too. I go to school with them, into town, everywhere. My friends call me 'Slim the Glider.'"

"And wind surfing?"

"No, that's for the petit bourgeois and the jerks."

"Jerks?"

"Yeah, the Parisians, I mean everyone who lives above the Loire River and who comes down here for our sun."

"You're exaggerating! There are people who are really good on their boards, aren't there?"

"Champions, people who do competition. The others are all petit bourgeois or jerks. Or both. Surfing, yeah, I would have liked it. But we don't have big waves here."

At night, a stronghold of immigrants. In the streets, piles of garbage between the parked cars. Almost no women on the

Of Dreams and Assassins

terraces of the Arab cafés. Men in groups drinking mint tea. Standing in groups at the intersections or "holding up the walls." Strolling along in twos, hand in hand. I feel like I'm back in Oran.

"What's the name of this neighborhood?"

"Plan Cabanes-Figuerolles."

"You'd think you were in North Africa."

"A lot of workers without families live in Sonacotra company housing or slum apartments. In the evening they all come here."

"Slim . . . I'm going to need your help."

"For?"

"I came here looking for someone. I know nothing about her except her first and last name."

"Are you crazy or what? How do you think you're going to find her?"

"I don't know yet."

"Are you at least sure that she lives here?"

"She told me that she lived in Montpellier. Twenty-four years ago . . . "

"Twenty-four years ago? I'm dreaming!"

"I'll call everyone in the telephone book with the same name. And the Minitel . . . does that thing work?"

"Yeah. Is it someone in your family?"

"No . . . it's too complicated . . . I'll explain it to you another time."

"But it's somebody from down there?"

"Yes."

"Well, old lady, that's going to be tricky. Immigrants don't all have telephones."

"We'll see. And especially inquire with the business owners, your acquaintances and friends . . . doesn't the grapevine work everywhere?"

"Faster than in the village, you can't imagine! With *ghurba* and its problems, like my mother says, the circuitry is under such tension that it makes its own blah-blah-blah all by itself. It often makes fights and *shikayas* . . . but I've never heard that it worked miracles! Hey, that's where I live."

Of Dreams and Assassins

I stop. He jumps out. Grabs his skateboard and then his moped:

"If it weren't late, I'd introduce you to my mother. She's always happy to talk about over there, especially with someone who's just arrived. She's worried about the country. But she's definitely already in bed at this hour. She works so much."

"Yes, she's undoubtedly sleeping."

"No, no, even when she's dead with fatigue, she doesn't sleep until I'm back. She lies down and waits for me."

"So hurry up and go in. That'll be for another time if you like. When can we see each other again?"

"Tomorrow I've got to work. I have an assignment to prepare. The day after tomorrow about six o'clock in Palavas?"

"Okay. Will you have gas this time?"

"Yeah, don't worry. On the first quay in the port?"

"Understood. Good night."

"Thanks for bringing me back. Hey, wait! What's the name of the person you're looking for?"

"Zana Baki. She's Algerian too."

"Zana Baki, doesn't ring a bell. A woman is more difficult to find. They live in hiding here as they do over there. It's their first I.D. card."

Behind me an impatient driver honks. I take off reluctantly.

"Later!" Slim yells to me.

Slim's departure returns me to my solitude. To the state of a foreigner in a foreign town. I try to go toward Place de la Comédie. Constantly run into one-way streets. Lose myself in neighborhoods unknown to me. Go around the city twice before managing to get oriented and reaching the center of town again.

I find once again the luxurious France and its mix of people. Around the esplanade the street lamps pour out phosphorescent light onto the greenery. Darkness lurks in the trees at the edges, transforming them into ghostly mastodons. A colorfully dressed crowd scatters onto the benches bordered by flower beds. The restaurants are still bustling. Montpellier, an inaccessible present time. I feel like a sleepwalker here. Cross it without being completely here. Too small to lose myself here and go beyond the limits of anguish. Too rich to be welcoming. Too uptight to allow for strolling. Its houses, its fancy apartment buildings . . . like as many cold dreams. Closed in by their self-sufficiency. I'm attracted by the sources of light. I bang against the windows like a fly. Like a fly caught in the trap of light barriers. False vistas. Behind the windows, temptations to which I can't succumb.

My point of view is distorted. I know. Suddenly, my solitude crushes and exhausts me. Despite the absence of obstacles and constraints, I feel imprisoned in the midst of this opulence and these excesses. I think of Oran with sadness. Oran, my *raï*, my insomnia. An anthill of devouring looks. Hopes devastated.

Fatigue has floored me. A profound sleep and, deep within it, nightmares. Unlike usual, I have no memory of them upon awakening. Just a fear drowned in the indecipherable. I stretch and leap up. The sun is streaming onto the sea. I prepare coffee and settle in on the balcony to have my breakfast. Set a rose purchased the night before in front of me and marvel at how the flavor of dishes can so change with the location. I have an appetite. The memory of Slim is a feast. Slim and Alilou are superimposed in my thoughts. The same joie de vivre makes them radiate. Gives grace to the smallest of their gestures. Catches on contagiously to those they approach. Two energies. Two Cartesian divers who dance like rays of light around the lives of others. That Slim had an unknown father brings him even closer to me, makes him almost necessary. Is it an effect of the homesickness and the solitude, like over there in the desert? I clung to him in a shameless way. Started pontificating in order to interest him. Until I was boring. But

Of Dreams and Assassins

even though I don't recognize myself in last night's behavior, I don't regret it. And I rejoice in advance at the idea of seeing this will-o'-the wisp again.

The next morning I decide to go immerse myself in this immigrant neighborhood. Just that—find out what its daytime atmosphere is like. For the moment, I have no strategy. And then, after twenty-five years of ignorance, there can't be any urgency about it.

Settled in front of a glass of tea, I let myself be carried away by the animation. An alternation between *raï* and Andalusian music in a store to my left. Verses from the Koran sung at the top of someone's lungs to my right. Richly colored cloth on display in another. Spices from the South and a sundry piling up of cassettes, dishes, pottery, suitcases, puff cushions . . . baskets of mint and coriander. And, to complete the atmosphere, the smoke from grilled merguez sausages, whose odor, in the long run, ends up making me nauseated.

I scrutinize the swarthy faces. Try desperately to remember Zana Baki's features. In vain. None of those faces awakens in me a memory. Only this sensation of women deported into the furthermost bounds of themselves. Of busy mothers out of my reach, far from my life. Numerous mothers. Shadows that go by and withdraw, leaving in me a vibration that oscillates between regret and rejection.

Two adolescents suddenly emerge from a building. After never-ending discussion and gesticulating, they head off toward the Cours Gambetta. A scholarly disorder of hair worked over with gel. Protruding muscles. Sassy looks. They bounce onto the other sidewalk. Beur caricatures. The sight of them annoys me. I look away.

I don't bury my nose again in my newspaper. I've read everything during the more than two hours I've been sitting there. Except for the classifieds. I order a fourth glass of tea. Chin in my hand, I look at Rue Faubourg-Figuerolles: poverty-stricken buildings. Loose doors. Dirty sidewalks. Two steps from the center of town, a third world where gypsies and immigrants hang around.

"The street cleaners, dressed in green, stop at the bottom of the Jardin Peyrou. You never see them on this side. The Cours Gambetta is a border," answers the owner of the tea salon, when I note out loud the garbage strewn about the neighborhood.

"You wouldn't have discouraged them a bit, by chance, would you?"

The man chokes with indignation. Flings the glass of tea in my face. I have to back up so as not to get splashed. He takes off with a furious look. His gestures make me laugh. Laughter that sounds so false that I immediately swallow it. My attempts at humor always end this way. Aggressiveness sticks to my skin. My pride bristles like barbed wire. It pokes others and tears me. Wounded and clawed like an Algerian woman. This should be a saying.

I go pay at the counter. Leave a big tip and in a conciliatory tone of voice ask the owner:

"Please, Si Mohamed, would you happen to know a woman by the name of Zana Baki?"

"May Allah's prayers and his peace be on Him. Is Baki the name of her husband or her father?"

"I don't know."

"Well you have to know! If you want to find a woman, look for her men."

They've changed countries for nothing—their psychology stays the same. The owner gives me a stealthy glance. I leave the premises.

Three men are dragging along in front of me and hug the walls as if they too wanted to make themselves invisible. Their eyes hardly see the French women passing by. They're undoubtedly unemployed workers if they're in the street at this hour. My heart tightens. Seeing me, they slow down. Stare at me. Stop. I do what I refused to do in Oran. I smile at them. My misfortune! Canine hunger immediately lights up their eyes. Rid of the arrogance with which they stare at women down there, the way they look at Maghrebian women here has something even more intolerable about it. A sort of morbid greed that lends them the expression of someone dying, of a vampire. Of someone dying and already changing into a vampire. Will we never have anything but that kind of rapport, even in exile? A flash of rage makes my muscles stiffen. My anger is stronger than their abjectness, greater than their frustrations. Now I want to be violent. Want to poke out the eyes that dare look at me in this way.

An old man has seen what's going on. He speaks to me.

"Continue on your way, my daughter. Go your way and forgive. Their whole life is a punishment."

I observe him. His face has the beauty of goodness. An indulgence that I picked up on here and there in the streets of Oran even when I made sure I was watching no one.

"Go your way and forgive." Three steps and I'm angry with myself for lapsing into such intolerance. For giving in to this anger that could be interpreted here as a racist reaction toward all Maghrebians. To overcome it I say to myself: I am free; they're locked into the blockhouses of tradition. Have been inside since the dawn of time. The dawn of ignorance. A time of suffering.

These virtuous thoughts don't calm me down. Reasoning can no longer help. My patience and compassion are exhausted.

Why did I come here this morning? Am I a masochist? Yet I had decided to offer myself a week of relaxation. Here I am again as tight as a knot from uneasiness and indignation.

"Go your way and forgive." "You're full of hate." Hatred of whom? Of what? Hatred or despair? Hatred and despair? Despair about dreaming, of all the broken dreams. One doesn't dream in a country like mine. Especially when one is a woman. One comes to terms with human blackness.

Of Dreams and Assassins

The skies of the South tire me. I've had enough of their lying blue color. Of their atmosphere of sweat, dust, tears, and blood. Of their tragic light. I need clouds. I need torment above and serenity on earth. I want a desert of snow and no longer to receive in my face only the cold of the wind. And in my eyes, a whiteness falling from the firmament.

Dreams of Two Souths

Standing facing the sea, his feet slightly apart in the water, a little boy holds an imaginary kite. He accompanies the circling of his arms with a "vroom" sound, sometimes slowly, sometimes faster. Then turning toward the beach:

"Mommy! Mommy! Mommy!"

A woman lifts her eyes from the book she's reading and focuses them on him.

"Mommy, look, I'm controlling the ocean!"

"My son, you're so strong!"

The little boy coos. Brings his eyes back to the ocean and starts up again with a noisy "vroom." His mother's look caresses his chubby little body for a long time, her smile tender, before she returns to her reading.

I look at this child and I see another. Alilou is nine years old. Has the complexion of Saharan kids. In his eyes burns a vast dream. I see the desert. Its war-blue sky. A white-hot *regg*. The air trembles and troubles the mind. In the distance a mirage shimmers. In this scintillating light, the *qsar*, prey of all excesses, resembles an anthill. Its ochre-colored walls merge into indigo blue. As if the sky had run off with the earth. As if there were nothing else left in the world but its absolute blueness.

A thousand leagues away from any habitation, I see that car, a four-wheel drive. How and why did it break down there? How long ago? It no longer has wheels, windows, an engine, or seats. A carcass cooked and recooked by the sun, scoured by the sand winds. It's Alilou's "sputnik." We use big rusted

Of Dreams and Assassins

oilcans for seats. Alilou has put together a steering wheel and a wooden "shaft."

"Hold on tight, we're going to burst through the sky!"

I curl up and grab onto the remains of the dashboard, taking care to avoid the torn-apart edges. Alilou wiggles around. Makes his "seat" grate on the car's sheet metal.

"Vroom-vroom-vroom, that's it, we've crossed it, look!"

I relax, turn toward him, and wait for what he's going to describe to me. Neither the desert nor this ghostly four-wheel drive have anything to do with it. It's his voice that transports me. I see with his words. With his marvelous words. And the fireflies dancing in the night of his eyes participate in the mystery.

"Look, from far away the earth looks like a sweet potato."

"A sweet potato?"

"Yes, an old potato. Look at that down there, it's the paradise planet. We're not gonna go there."

"Why, isn't it beautiful?"

"Whew! It's all gray with boredom. There's just people praying: 'Allah! Allah! Allah!' They're so dull that they'd make a dog fall asleep in his own crap. There aren't any heroes or funny people, or people who commit sins. You have to go to the devil's place in hell to find those people."

I burst out laughing:

"Make a dog fall asleep in his own crap?"

"Haven't you ever heard that at home? My mother always says it about fools, idiots who annoy her. Shall we go to hell? I want to show you some things."

I tremble with fear:

"No, no, please, don't take me to hell!"

Then he laughs. Whatever the intonation, his voice is melodious. Alilou quickly becomes serious again and shoots a furious look at me:

"You swallow all the silly things people tell you. It's great at the devil's place in hell! There are all the Tintins, the Popeyes, the Blek le Rocs, the Tartines, the Goldoracs, the Djehas, and the Targous of the world. There are all the singers, the storytellers, the jokers . . . Every day is a celebration. And the devil is the cleverest of the clowns and magicians. The prophets are very jealous of him, because he is Allah's darling."

"And who told you that?"

"Allah."

"Allah?"

"Yes, Allah. I went to see him on his star. He told me he was sick, really sick of Muslims. They haven't left him in peace since Muhammad the First. He says they're sick from praying. 'Allah, Allah, Allah, Allah . . .' So it's ended up being an epidemic. It's screwed up their heads. Allah's fed up with their *'baraka'* and their *'inshallah.'* They think that with that, Allah will do everything for them. Do you realize that they call him one hundred billion billion times a second? If he were to listen to them, he'd never have the time to take care of others in the world."

We burst out laughing. Suddenly a question comes to my mind. In this case, does paradise or hell await my father? Alilou has put my mind in a whirl. I'm no longer sure to which beyond I should doom my progenitor.

"What's the matter with you? Are you still scared of hell? I'll drop you off on your damned desert immediately if you like! You know what, the desert is a nightmare of misfortune. Life is true hell."

"I know. That's why they send me here. Vacation is the sea. It's for other people. I'm always punished because I don't have a mother."

"So what?"

"So nothing, you can go on."

After all, I'm not going to tell him what's bothering me. And anyway, I don't want to ruin these moments.

A few months later, a dream more powerful than the others carried Alilou away. Abandoning his "sputnik," embedded in the sand, he left, driven by his thirst for life and discovery.

"Alilou, where are you running off to like that?" a neighbor apparently asked him that day.

"To see what's over there, far away, behind the sky's roof. And this time I'm going on foot."

Of Dreams and Assassins

In the *douar*, no one was surprised anymore by this raga-muffin's excesses. Pensive, the neighbor watched Alilou as he moved away. He would have liked to have been of the age to share the games of this Aladdin. With nostalgia, the man ended up turning away and slowly continuing on his path toward the *qsar*.

That night, Alilou did not return home at dinnertime. Anxious, his mother and father went looking for him. Found him nowhere. Since the *douar* had no electricity, the inhabitants made a big fire outside to help guide the rascal in the dark. Armed with oil lamps, the men left in groups of two to search the vicinity. The four-wheel carcass was empty. The calls were lost in a muffled calmness. Without echoes, without responses.

Soon a violent sandstorm developed, forcing the men to turn around and go back. They assembled at the house of the little boy's parents. The women made tea. Everyone drank in silence. They listened gloomily to the screams of the storm. The sand's claws scraped *reggs* and *hamadas*. Combed the darkness. A terrible omen from the skies. One never sweeps after someone's departure. He would risk never returning. And then, this cosmic breath will leave no further trace of the child. In order to ward off ill fortune, Alilou's mother prayed. From time to time she opened the courtyard door and threw a little water onto the wind's hysteria. Watering, on the other hand, augurs well. A life link between those remaining and the one leaving.

The next day, when the sandy whirlwinds had calmed down, they of course found no indication of the boy's destination. Even later, no nomad, no shepherd ever discovered his body.

At that time, I was up north. Unaware of what had happened to my friend. I was to find out only two months later when I returned to the desert for Easter vacation.

Of Dreams and Assassins

Slanderers affirmed that Allah had wanted to punish the imp for his sacrilegious "frenzies." The man who saw and spoke to Alilou last, a man as learned as he was pious, tried to soothe his mother with words of consolation. "Don't listen to ordinary people. The narrowness of their judgment is an offense to God's grandeur. What they call a frenzy is the privilege of vivacious minds. Telling stories is a divine gift that is becoming more and more rare. And your son was a born storyteller. You know that the sand wind fascinated him. I remember one day he said to me: 'When there's a sand wind, it's Allah moving about with his star.' God sent him a fantastic sand wind to call him back to him. Alilou is not dead. He has gone to the realm of eternal childhood. He is among the angels, with the chosen people."

"Gone to the realm of eternal childhood," this sentence softened my pain. Why hadn't he waited to take me with him? The richness of his language and his imagination, with its flamboyance, had until then given shape to and clothed the nudity of these immense desert spaces. Without him, I fell back into "the true living hell," as he liked to call the desert. I was once again caught between two states of aridity, of sand and of silence.

No other child could replace in my eyes or in my heart this live wire. I withdrew further into myself and into the memory of him. Subsequently, only fictional heroes, Peter Pan, the Little Drummer, the Little Prince, and other elves led me down the same paths as his. At the end of the day, when the heat was a little less scorching, I would go, book in hand, and lean against the front of the four-wheel-drive carcass. Sometimes the characters in my readings, out of the blue, would take on Alilou's voice. I would abruptly turn around to face the car. Wasn't I going to discover him behind me, at the wheel of his sputnik? At that moment, it seemed to me that I heard, bursting forth out of the silence, the crystal-clear and mocking laughter of my friend. And I always had the feeling that I saw him skimming the sands like a little whirlwind.

Of Dreams and Assassins

My eyes are filled with the vision of the sea. Its expanse covers and erases the desert. The blond child splashes about in the water. His mother has joined him. She takes him under the arms and tries to teach him to swim. His little cries are a mix of fright and joy. I am alone and well.

Tight jeans folded up at the ankles. His shirt in the wind. The movement of his arms matching that of his legs, Slim arrives on skates. Before even stopping, he cries out:

"Wow, a Swan! A beautiful beast."

From his look I understand that he's talking about the boat I'm facing.

"I know absolutely nothing about it."

"It's a Swedish boat. Bridge and interior made of teak. Luxury model. With that, you can rush along and cut through the waters of any sea, with your eyes closed. I've never seen that one here. Hey, a Panamanian flag, a lucky devil passing through . . . What'd you do yesterday?"

"I didn't want to go into town. During the day I went swimming and walked on the beach. Then in the village I met an old *pied-noir* from Oran. The handle of her bag broke. Tomatoes and lemons rolled onto the sidewalk. I helped her pick them up. She stared at me for a long time before saying: 'You're from home.' When she found out I was from Oran, she invited me to drink a pastis. We talked about our city for a long time. Her neighbors, also *pieds-noirs,* joined us. Only now do I realize what trauma they went through."

"For sure. But some of them closed themselves off in their pain. Transformed it into hatred. Thirty years later, they still understand nothing about history."

"That's because history crushed their destiny."

"Yes, but even so . . . fortunately there are some really great ones."

"That's the case with the *pieds-noirs* I've spoken to except for one. He told me that the people who 'threw him out' had

Of Dreams and Assassins

'nothing to do in France!' That he'd be quite able in his turn to take a gun to turn them back. 'We left them the country and look what they've done with it,' he added with rage."

"Yeah! We know who he votes for."

"In the evening I had a drink at the edge of the canal. I met a Palavas regular, an accordionist named Bambino . . . "

"Bambino's a star."

"He has a funny accent."

"He's from Sèteu! Did he sing Brassens to you and talk about his rival, the black widow?"

"Yes, yes, and the rest . . . When I returned, I read late into the night. I'm trying to live normally. To escape from anguish. It's really odd for me to be here."

"'Mets de l'huile' on the terrors of Algiers. Let yourself go."

"And you, your homework assignment?"

"Great! . . . I learned something that's going to make you very happy."

"Tell me quickly."

"I asked my mother how to go about trying to find an Algerian woman who has been living here for twenty years and about whom you only know the name. I explained everything to her. Well, the little you told me. My mother thinks that it shouldn't be very complicated in this case."

"Oh yeah? Not complicated? Why?"

"It just so happens that right next to our house, a Moroccan woman, Khalti Aïcha, has a fabric boutique for Arabic women. It seems she's had it for thirty years. And before that she was the only one in the region to sell these fabrics."

"So?"

"So, inevitably, all the Maghrebian women shop at her boutique. My mother says that at that time there weren't many Maghrebian women in Montpellier. It's only been in the last ten or fifteen years that they've been joining their men here. She says that if your Zana Baki has really been here for more than twenty years, then Khalti Aïcha must surely know her."

"You think so?"

"If my mother says so . . . You must be as lucky as the devil."

My heart starts pounding in my chest. Sitting on the edge of the quay, I feel myself fainting. Had I stayed standing, my legs would have given out under me. Slim notices my emotion. "Hey, you're feeling sort of out of it. What's happening to you?"

"I don't know. It's suddenly so quick. Too quick. It surprises me."

"You're looking for your mother. Is that it?"

"No, no. My mother died a long time ago."

"So who's this woman?"

I give a rough sketch of my story. Now Slim's eyes wander onto the boats without seeing them. He seems puzzled.

"Is it your turn to feel out of it?"

"How did that get hold of you after all this time? I don't understand what you hope to find . . . Are people already senile at age thirty?"

"That's how it is. In certain cases you can't cover up something that is beyond your understanding, and yet, it doesn't stop bothering you. One day, you finally give in and want to know. Just that: to know. If you succeed. Try to fill an empty space with a story. For lack of anything better."

"Yeah . . . as for me, I don't bother with such stories. It's all drivel. What counts is reality. Reality doesn't bother me."

"Hm."

"What do you mean, 'hm'? Do you see me running all the way to Mali for a guy who never cared about my mother and me? Frankly! And what can that bring me? A tribe of one-hundred-percent Malian half brothers and sisters. Nothing to brag about. Besides, they're the ones who are likely to come after me one day. Misery down there, luxury here, and Slim wearing the skin of a SON OF FRANCE, a rich son, you know, since my mother often brushes up against the RMI. 'My son, my brother, how we missed you!' And the endless exaggerated politeness of the Africans. As if we had just left each other a few weeks earlier. Do you see my mother and me cleaned out by the Algerian and Malian tribes? They would scrape us to the bone."

"What I see is that it's already eating at you."

Of Dreams and Assassins

"What's eating at me is that I don't ever want to know them. Don't mix things up! Besides, when I reach legal age, in two years, I'll take MY MOTHER'S name and French nationality. I'm the son of a lone woman. And proud of it. And that's enough for me. Anyway, I'll tell you: I feel completely French."

"Hey, I thought you were made of three halves."

"Oh, the other two are just so I don't deny who I am, and especially for my mother, who holds on to her roots. For me, I drag along the Algerian and the Malian origins like cooking pans. Havoc and wind. And my mother's sighs. Nothing more than that."

"Hm."

"Stop with your 'hms.' They annoy me. I know what's going on in your head. You're thinking that with the years I'll have time to change my mind."

"Exactly."

"You're a kamikaze of misfortune! I love life too much to go throwing it and myself into problems I don't have. I'll leave by boat. I'll go see countries that only have origins in my dreams of travel. Where I'll put down moorings that are ready to be cast off. I won't go looking for melodrama, problems, and roots. My only origin is my mother's womb. And even from that you're expelled so you can be born and live. So for all the rest, the hell with it!"

"I don't like this word 'origin.' In today's world it serves all causes. All exclusions. I just want to know who my mother was. How she lived. Can't you understand that? . . . But we'll talk about it later. Shall we go?"

"By boat? I'd gladly take that one!"

"You know very well where I want to go."

"To Khalti Aïcha's? There's no fire."

"I'm going there right away, with or without you."

"I would have done better to have kept my mouth shut a bit. You don't even give me time to eye the boats."

"You have your whole life ahead of you for that."

"And as for you, it was years before you began to worry about your Zana Baki. So that can certainly wait one more hour."

Of Dreams and Assassins

To cut short the procrastination, I get up and go toward the parking lot where I parked the Méhari. After a second, Slim catches up with me. Makes circles around me on his skates: "You're too much."

"Get in."

"I left my moped on the other side of the canal so I could skate."

"We'll go get it."

"My mother said you could come and have dinner at the house if you want."

"I won't say no."

"I think she wants to see what you look like so she can feel reassured about who I'm hanging around with . . . Sometime I might let some crazy chick get her claws into me."

He glances at me sideways. I shrug my shoulders. Slapping his thigh, he bursts out laughing.

"No, no it's not true. My mother doesn't have a twisted mind. She has a MONSTER NOSTALGIA. My mother aches for her country. Like you, Mamma mia, the two of you are not simply going to treat me to images with your talk of the other side. This evening, I think I'm clearly going to be shown a film. Without intermission. With tears and handkerchiefs."

"You don't miss anything, do you?"

Despite the impatience that makes me accelerate more than I should, his giggles are contagious. I really do have the luck of the devil to have met this elf who pirouettes between his roots like he does on his city's pavement.

Words Like Sequins

In the midst of her shimmering cloth, her clothes are modern. A pleated skirt falls to the middle of her calf. Matching blouse and vest. A scarf knotted into a headband at her temple, her eyes blackened with kohl and a mischievous look contrast sharply with the plainness of her clothing. Give her the look of a sorceress, searching in vain to hide it by the restraint in her clothing. The coquette is on the far side of fifty.

"Hello, Khalti Aïcha."

"Slimou! Hello, my son. Hello, mademoiselle. Are you the one looking for Zana from Oran?"

And without waiting for my answer, she speaks to Slim:

"Your mother told me. We had tea together before she went to work. Speaking of tea, I have some hot. Do you want some?"

"Oh yes, Khalti Aïcha!" exclaims Slim greedily.

The woman disappears into the back of her store. I look daggers at Slim.

"Don't be in such a hurry! You've seen how the grapevine works! And this time not for *menshar*. That's rare."

Since I haven't answered, he adds as an excuse:

"Khalti Aïcha needs to sweeten her palate in order to talk. Without that she doesn't loosen up, and you'll see, she's really the queen of tea. It's not tea with mint, it's mint with tea. And what mint!"

The woman returns with a tray in her hands.

"So you know Zana Baki?"

"It's normal that Maghrebians have to go to Arab cloth merchants and butchers. They can buy all the rest somewhere else.

Except that. And in the past there were only two butchers and only me for cloth. You'd have to say there weren't many of us. That's how it is. In earlier times, we were France's apprentices at home. Now we play that role here. And there are some who dare say we're colonizing France."

A burst of laughter.

"Khalti Aïcha, you're nobody's apprentice. Your hands only touch the fluorescence of feast days."

Aïcha takes it all in. Envelops Slim with a tender look. Then begins talking with me again:

"I knew three Zanas during the period that concerns you. One from Marrakech, one from the Sahara, and one from Oran. But I haven't seen the Oranian for a long time."

"Do you know where she lives?"

"She was living in La Paillade. In Grand Mail, I think. But I don't know if she's still there. She was very sick about a year ago. I went to see her in the hospital. I haven't seen her again since. You know how it is, work and all. You run, you run, and you never have time. And she must not have gone to Algeria this summer. Otherwise she would have come and stocked up for her family at my shop."

"I hope she's not dead."

"No, no, may Allah ward off calamity. I would have known that."

Suddenly a light goes on in my mind. How is it I hadn't thought of it earlier? Everything is buzzing inside of me and disconnects me.

"But tell me, in that case maybe you also knew Keltoum Meslem, a friend of Zana's."

"*Meskina!*"

"You knew her?!"

"*Meskina!* She's dead. A long time ago and in a sad way. After all, there's no happy death . . . But even so . . . "

Shrillness. The flashes of light from the cloth are like slivers piercing my eyes.

"Here, sit down."

Slim moves a chair toward me. I let myself drop into it. The woman, intrigued, scrutinizes me:

"Why are you talking about Keltoum? Who are you?"

"Her daughter."

"*Ya rebbi! Ya rebbi!*"

She rests her elbows on the counter. Her face in her hands, she observes me with consternation.

"My goodness!"

A period of silence before she starts speaking again:

"Now that you say so, I think you look like her."

"Really, I look like her?"

"Yes, you're her image!"

"Why do you say she died sadly?"

Aïcha straightens up uneasily. Begins folding and unfolding the cloth on her counter. Gives me a glance from which all mischievousness has disappeared.

"One can't speak about that in a store and in front of a grown boy."

"Oh, I can leave if you want."

And so saying, Slim quickly swallows his second glass of tea.

"You're going to strangle yourself drinking like a *khbayti* sucking on his bottle. No hurry. We'll talk tonight. I prefer that."

Then addressing me:

"Come have supper with me. I'm not far from here. Slim will bring you. We can talk in peace."

"She's invited to our house."

"Then tell your mother that I'll come too. You'll leave us alone for a moment, my son."

"Okay, Khalti Aïcha."

She holds out a glass to me:

"Here, drink your tea my daughter. Your mother suffered a lot. A very good woman. She thought about you all the time. She cried and wailed: 'If I'd known, I would have stolen her the one time I was able to see her again. She was two years old. But I wanted to do things legally.' Your father never allowed her to see you again. She had taken some steps to take this right away from him. He let things drag on and never answered the summons. She planned on taking you away and

Of Dreams and Assassins

keeping you permanently. But when she went to Oran, she couldn't find you. Your father must have hidden you."

"Yes."

"Too bad, death took Keltoum away! And so young, *meskina*."

Absolute silence in my head. Whirling of lights! Farandoles of joy easing my pain. I drink a sip of tea to regain my composure. My hands are trembling. My glass of tea is trembling. Fabrics swirling. The woman smiles at me compassionately.

"It's dried mint from the desert. An elixir. Friends bring it to me. To make people laugh, I tell them it's to reach seventh heaven."

She tries to take on a light-hearted tone. Her eyes keep a seriousness mixed with surprise.

"Aïcha, please talk to me about her."

Despite my pleading voice, Aïcha resists:

"This evening, my daughter, this evening. And to tell the truth, I don't know much. Zana will be able to inform you better than me. I'll tell her you're here. She'll be very happy and will immediately show up. Your mother and she were inseparable."

Why this reticence? I ready myself to try to squeeze out of her what she's not telling me when a man comes into the store.

"Salaam, Aïcha. *Bojor, bojor,*" he says to us.

"Welcome, Ahmed. What brings you here?"

"My sister's being married in the village. I have to take some cloth with me. But I don't know anything about women's clothes."

The man begins nosing around cautiously. Aïcha goes toward him, obviously relieved that she can escape my questions.

"'*Soutège.*' Some say *souffège,* 'wild.' Two tones of pink and two of blue."

The man moves about. Takes out other rolls of cloth.

"'Boudiaf' and 'Chadli's mustaches,' *chlarem Chadli.* Those are no longer fashionable and for good reason."

A hint of annoyance shows in the man's eyes:

"How can they put Boudiaf on the same level as Chadli?

Of Dreams and Assassins

People respect nothing any longer! And why not Ali Bel Hadj, while they're at it?"

"Oh that, that's not possible. Even transformed into cloth, that one would have barked. Can you imagine that, cloth that barks like a dog, rips apart all by itself, and blows up your shop?"

"Aïcha! 'They' have their spies, even here."

"Spies or not, here they hide in their pubic hair like lice."

"Aïcha, be careful of what you say. I'm a friend."

"So, friend, I'm counting on you to come and resuscitate me if 'they' were to kill me. With a first name like mine, you should be able to manage!"

"If you were threatened, all the neighborhood men would mobilize to defend you. You know that. Whatever happens, your 'Chadli's mustaches,' I wouldn't take it if you gave it to me."

"I have something better to sell you. Here, this is 'woven,' *mensuj*. I have it in gold and silver. Here, you've got different lamés."

"And what's that?"

"Crocheted, *krushi*. No, it's not possible. Do you want me to believe you don't even know that!"

"When it comes to women's things, I'm a poor ignoramus."

Aïcha comes back with an unambiguous "that's the truth." And continues:

"That's 'your eyes, oh your eyes,' *'aynik ya 'aynik.*"

She said that as she slowly shook her head. Her eyes are once again mischievous. Furthermore, it's her eyes that the man stares at intensely. Swaying her hips, Aïcha comes back to the main counter. Serves him a glass of tea. Explains about the same piece of cloth:

"City people also call it 'Madonna.' The peasants, the *'aru-biyya*, say 'beans,' *lubya*, because of the shape of the sequins. Each one sees what he can. Allah alone watches all of us."

Slim makes a concerted effort not to burst out laughing. The man rubs one of his cheeks. His eyes linger more and more on Aïcha. The coquette, who seems used to the effects of her charms, takes wicked pleasure in allowing herself to be admired. Despite the impatience keeping me on tenterhooks, the spiciness of the scene has me captivated.

"This one?"

"'The brother of girls,' *akhu al banat,* a beautiful satin. Touch this softness for me. And thick, too. Next to it you have 'the leaden brother of women.'"

"Hm, appropriate. At home they're filling brothers with bullets."

"Back home they're filling them with lead and decapitating girls and mothers too. After subjecting them to all the vile acts you know about."

"No more respect . . . This one?"

"'Sugar,' *essocar,* a speckled chiffon. Here, 'it's falling in downpours,' *issob m'rrachrach.* There, 'I'm going up to have myself photographed,' *talâ netsaouar.*"

Slim can't prevent himself any longer from chuckling:

"They put all the drama and fantasy missing in their lives in words. Even to name cloth! It's incredible!"

Her index finger on her lips, Aïcha turns toward him, and she couldn't be more serious. She's not joking. She's working.

Slim comes toward me and whispers in my ear:

"A real pro. Have you seen how she sets about doing it? The guys lose their money!"

I agree. Aïcha continues:

"Here you have 'Dallas' and 'Cable TV.' I have them in all colors."

The laughter that Slim stifles once more shakes his body and makes his eyes sparkle.

"All of this seems good. Help me, I don't know what I should buy."

"If you want my opinion, start with solid values. You won't be disappointed by women's reactions back home."

"And what are 'solid values'?"

"Calais lace. Guipure. 'Love velvet,' *hâtifète el houa.*"

The man gives her a meaningful look. She takes advantage of it. Immediately rolls open the bolts she's just pointed out.

"How much do you want?"

"Four 'love velvets.' They'll make caftans."

Of Dreams and Assassins

"God be praised. Now you're finding your wits for 'women's things' again."

"Memory and happiness are women. Forgetting and unhappiness, too. I'm not going to teach you that. Aïcha . . . give me material for two dresses from each of the others, too. In short, just follow your own instinct. I'll leave it up to you."

Aïcha comes back to her counter satisfied. Measures and cuts pieces of cloth. Piles them up.

"Ahmed, can I ask you a favor?"

"I would give you my eyes."

She smiles and pulls her scarf a little further toward her saucy eyes.

"Please don't put that in a Tati bag."

"Why?"

"I'll get pimples on my face as big as that," and she holds up her fist.

"I'd be upset with myself for spoiling such beauty. It shall be done according to your wishes, *ya lalla*."

"Thank you, Ahmed."

He takes out a wad of bills and pays. Can't stop looking at Aïcha.

"I'll come to see you as soon as I get back."

"That's fine. Come buy some more 'love velvet,' Madonna, and Dallas. You'll see, your women will ask for more."

Since he remains planted there, she adds a phrase to get him to leave:

"Good-bye, may peace be with you, and *baraka* with this marriage."

He takes his package.

"Salaam."

And leaves regretfully. Aïcha watches him leave. As soon as he's crossed the threshold of her shop, she exclaims:

"It's his daughter that he's marrying off, not his sister. For goodness sake, he takes me for an idiot! 'An ignoramus concerning women's things,' *zaa'ma*. They all say that each time so I'll repeat these names. It excites them. As long as they keep buying."

"Khalti Aïcha, those fabric names are fantastic."

Of Dreams and Assassins

"Slimou, my son, in our past misery, we had only that; words in the wind of voices. We sold nothing. We bartered supplies and stories. Stories in order to live. The habit remains."

"Yeah, but now your words have sequins. And bread in the end."

"Bread?"

"Money, money, Khalti Aïcha."

"Have you seen how our kids born here talk? Their heads are *francis*. All the way down to their belly buttons! Obviously, Arabic below that . . ."

"Do you deplore the fact that they're French?"

"No! Each to his own time. And then I'm going to tell you, even if France has barking dogs, you have to admit that we're better off than back home. RMI, free health care for the poor, whether they're Tunisian, Moroccan, Algerian, or *khoroto, rahma*, my daughter. Hey, the ones treated like miscreants show themselves to be closer to Allah than the ones committing massacres in His name, down there."

I have just had time to return to the subject that interests me when another customer comes into the shop. Aïcha says to me:

"Go, go and walk around a bit, my daughter. This is when I work the most. When the masons and *zufris*, returning from construction sites, come and do their shopping. I'll see you later."

"What time do you close?"

"Not before eight-thirty in the evening. Sometimes I'm still here after nine. Slim knows."

The adolescent agrees and invites me to follow him. Aïcha is already in an endless discussion with her client. I pick up my bag and reluctantly join Slim in the street.

"At seven-thirty we can go to my place. My mother ought to be home so she can prepare the grub."

"Let's let her do it in peace. I need a strong drink."

"What?"

"Whiskey."

"Do you want to unleash a revolution in the neighborhood?"

Of Dreams and Assassins

"Revolution . . . I wasn't able to make one at home . . . I just want some whiskey. Let's leave the immigrant *douar*, go to a French square. La Comédie?"

"Yeah, it's better. But you know, Montpellier is one big *douar*. You always see the same faces at La Comédie."

Sitting with our drinks before us, we don't manage to say a word. I'm grateful to him for his self-restraint at such a moment. The imminence of what I'm going to learn is like a trembling in my mind.

In the crowd of passersby, I suddenly notice the man who had spoken to me the day before yesterday in this same café. He has seen me too. Comes over:

"Good evening, are you doing well?"

"Yes, thank you, and you?"

"Very well. Have you become used to pleasure?"

"I'm trying."

"You still seem overwhelmed."

"Not for the same reason."

"Sit down, since you know each other."

Adding a gesture to his words, Slim pulls a wicker chair toward our table, and speaking to me, adds:

"I told you it's the *douar* here."

The man raises an eyebrow a little, hesitates, and asks me:

"May I?"

"Please."

"My name is Roger Faure."

"Kenza Meslem."

"I thought you knew each other."

We answer with the same wordless smile. Slim's eyes go from one to the other with a bit of a boorish look. The man's eyes, staring at him, force him to introduce himself too.

"Slim the Glider."

"The glider?"

Slim lifts a leg up and shows him his skates.

"Ah!"

Of Dreams and Assassins

"Excuse my indiscretion the other day. I don't think there are many men capable of resisting the tears of a foreign woman."

"You cried in public? Why?"

"Oh, just a tear. Maybe from delight. But the eyes of a lookout were roaming about."

"I had just gotten in from Algeria . . ."

"Just what I suspected. The urge to confirm it was burning my lips. That's what made me approach you. I got the opposite result. You fled. And I'm doing it again."

"No, no, I had to leave."

"I worked for a few years in Algeria. I like the country and its people. What's happening there upsets me."

"Where were you?"

"In Algiers. I was teaching biology at the university. And you?"

"Until last June, I was at the Faculty of Letters in Oran."

"Were you threatened?"

"No. At least not directly."

"I suppose you've contacted the Algerians who've taken up residence in Montpellier."

"No. Are there many?"

"Quite a few. They keep coming."

He takes a flier from his pocket and hands it to me. Various associations are having a meeting tomorrow night on the situation in Algeria.

"Will you come?"

"I don't know."

The man is surprised by my answer. Since I don't want to explain, I change my response:

"Probably."

"Hey, the sea."

Our eyes land on Slim. His thumb pointed back, he explains.

"It's a sea breeze."

In the sky, clouds push around the indigo blue of the sunset. The air has become moist.

With a roguish face, Slim seems to be unabashedly amusing himself at our expense. What's he thinking? What story is he making up?

"Are you from the other side too?"

"The ones who cross over don't glide. They're broken."

The man observes him with interest.

"That's right. So you're a Beur then?"

"Yuck! I hate that word. And I don't like butter either. It's sticky, it stains, and it becomes rancid."

I want to ask Slim: Have you finished directing the conversation? I realize that he's engaged in a new seduction campaign. He has succeeded in attracting the man's attention.

* * *

She has the dignity of those women who have managed with and against everyone. And "cleanly," as witnessed by her hands, which she brandishes like banners. No sting seems to torture her conscience. She has the peaceful weariness arrived at through duty accomplished. She is proud of her son. Shows it and says it with the same delight as her scatterbrain when he affirms that she is "UNIQUE." She calls him *kahlouchi*, "my dark one." He says *mima* or "old lady" with a little face as sparkling as a picture. Irresistible.

Even though it needs a little fixing up, the staircase is clean. "The outside door closes. And there's even an intercom!" mother and son say in chorus. Before laughing together about "these chic nothings" compared with the conditions of life of most of the other immigrants in the neighborhood. In the apartment there is a mixture of here and the other side. And I smell fragrances that make my mouth water.

"I made lasagna for a change from what you eat at home. I hope you like it at least?"

"I love it!"

"While we're waiting for Aïcha, would you like an aperitif?"

Watching for my reaction, Slim is delighted at my astonished look:

"What do you think? My mother's got culture. Hey, but she doesn't have any whiskey. Don't go overboard."

"No, but I have some port. A drop does you good every so

often. A long time ago, a Portuguese friend brought me some from her country. She was so disappointed when I told her I didn't drink that I tasted some. I thought it was good. But I also have pastis for friends. Allah who created us can't punish us for liking a few good things in life."

"Just a glass of water, please, Khadidja."

We talk about Algeria. Overwhelmed, she shakes her head.

"Before, those down there felt sorry for us, 'the poor émigrés, far from their country,' and so on and so forth. Now they envy us. And if only all we had to do was pity them! Their terror has crossed the sea. We clutch our stomachs whenever the phone rings late at night. We're in despair for that country in all of its self-destruction."

It's close to ten o'clock when Aïcha finally arrives. She plops down on a bench. Massages her legs, her neck. Her eyes are dreamy.

"I haven't stopped thinking about you since a while ago. Afterward, I had the impression that a ghost had visited. Your mother was even a little younger than you when she died. You had a strange effect on me."

Strange, yes. For her "ghost" is coming to me for the first time. For the first time, this strange feeling that she's no longer a ghost disinherited in the streets of Montpellier. That Aïcha's words have caused her to be reborn in me. The absent woman now has my face and my silhouette. She is a dead part in my life. And my mourning is being constructed with the words of others. With the weight of its nevers, remains of always.

Slim comes out of the kitchen with a small tray in his hands:

"I'm going to eat in my room so I can leave you to your whispering."

When he disappears, Aïcha says:

"A fine boy."

Then with a tired smile:

"You've really become old when you persist in thinking of strapping young men as children."

Of Dreams and Assassins

She takes off her shoes. Puts her legs up onto the bench. Sits cross-legged, her elbows on her knees and her face in her hands:

"What should I tell you about your mother except her death?"

I hold my breath. Khadidja puts down the plate of lasagna in front of us on the *meyda.*

"It's burning hot. It'd be better to wait before starting."

She realizes that Aïcha and I are staring at each other silently. Sits down and puts an arm around me. Aïcha turns away and begins speaking:

"Zana had been away in Marseilles for a few days. She telephoned your mother several times but was unable to reach her. Keltoum was never away. Her brother had been dead for three or four years already. She had no one in France. Zana also knew in what state her friend was. She shortened her stay. Upon her return she went directly to your mother's place. Nothing. She called for the neighbors who smashed down the door. On her side, her hands joined between her thighs and her knees to her chin, your mother was lying in a pool of blood. She had been dead for two or three days. *Meskina,* she'd become pregnant. And that was why Zana had gone to Marseilles, to look for help. Now there's the pill. And even if you find yourself trapped, there are clinics where doctors do that like it should be done. But before, it was forbidden. And what's even more dramatic is that we Maghrebian women don't know anything. The taboos of our education hold us down much more than the laws. We're silenced and fettered by shame."

"Who performed the abortion? Do you know?"

"No, we found out nothing. Maybe she did it all alone with a knitting needle. Zana thinks so. The doctors who saw her body said her uterus was punctured."

Khadidja squeezes me a bit harder. Brings my head onto her chest and rocks me. I realize that my forearms are pressing painfully against my abdomen.

"Do you know who the father was?"

Of Dreams and Assassins

"Me, no. Zana must undoubtedly know. But what does it matter?"

What matters to me is less the man than what my mother could have felt for him. Did she love him, if even only for a few hours? I'll ask Zana this question.

"How did she live?"

"Like all women alone here: during the day, housework for the French. In the evening, pride and bitterness in solitude. For the funeral and the repatriation of the body, the solidarity of the women certainly played a part. But the truth is the truth, Zana paid out almost all the expenses."

"The lasagna is going to get cold," observes Khadidja, without letting go of me.

I'm no longer hungry. Have Aïcha's words filled me or emptied me? I don't know. Salutary and tolerable brutality, thanks to the warmth of these women. We fall silent. The rain begins whipping the windowpanes. Infinite tenderness of mothers, daughters, and sisters with each other. This link that makes our women strong as a result of their defeats.

"There's one more thing that you must know: your mother tried to commit suicide after she had to leave you in order to return here. It seems a miracle that she pulled through that time. I don't know anything more. Zana will tell you."

Toward Other White Lands

It's raining cats and dogs. Wiping out the road. Hits my face and my eyes. Splatters from everywhere. Makes my clothes stick to my skin. The Méhari is like a small boat in the storm. I glide between two floods—my thoughts and the waters.

No light at the windows of the apartment building. As if the last inhabitants have gone, abandoning it like a shipwrecked freighter. A wreck washed up in rough weather. The ocean is rolling its anger against the sides. Gnawing at the beach. Crashing in my eardrums. Palavas seems like the outer confines of the world. A small island abandoned to this night's thundering assaults.

At my apartment, I change my clothes and serve myself a whiskey. Pace in circles. Can't imagine the other shore. I'm adrift. This evening's pandemonium deepens distance and time. Confuses my mind. Encloses me in an impenetrable solitude. Lamine, Selma, Foued, Kamel, Rachid . . . I suddenly remember that this morning in Algeria was the beginning of classes in the public schools and the universities! Haven't read the papers or listened to the news. A pain is cutting into my guts. I look at the telephone and my watch: midnight. Over there, my friends aren't sleeping. We're all like that now: insomniacs at night, sleepwalkers during the day. I dial Selma's number.

"Good evening, Selma."

"Kenza, how are you? Do you like it there? Kenza, they burned down the El Hayat lycée!"

"No way!"

Of Dreams and Assassins

"Yes, yes, and it's not going to stop there."

"And the beginning of classes?"

"Well, we still began, even so. Fear in the pit of our stomachs, but we went. And did you see? Nobody said on French TV that it was incredible proof of resistance on the part of an entire populace! Just to send one's children to school in spite of all the threats hanging over the beginning of the school year!"

"Of course . . . do you think it's the sign of an impending revolt on the part of the people?"

"Cattle!"

I burst out laughing. That devil Selma, she knows only contradiction. I hear her also laughing on the other end:

"I'm exaggerating as usual. I'd like it so much if people would get off their butts. How long are we going to take it? Other than the anger that explodes during demonstrations, there's nothing. We fall back into fear. Cattle! It's true you know!"

Kamel and Rachid are there, too. Then I call Lamine. He reads out names. Gone, disappeared, threatened, killed. Sad old chorus from times of hatred. But hearing the voices, especially the laughter of my friends, does me good. Laughter that breaks our silence. Disarms fear and derision. Relieves anguish. Laughter, our only weapon against what is loathsome. Laughter, foam of tears, between screaming and aphasia. An escape from asphyxiation. Laughter, trills, boasting about life when dreams are dying. An outburst in order to escape from drowning. And alcohol so as to forget, for an instant, that there's no respite. No forgetting.

I am a ghost. I'm wandering in the ruins of Oran. Beneath a sky of blood. There is no longer a single woman, nor a single child. There is no trace of them among these fallen rocks. They've turned into debris, burned from memory. There are only men, not quite men. No faces. No lower limbs. Live torsos that wriggle about in a chaos of rubble. Their heads are covered with eyes. Eyes staring hard in every direction. I say to myself: fortunately, I'm invisible. They can't see me. I'm just a glance. They can't seize me. I'm just the vapor from a

Of Dreams and Assassins

breath. All of a sudden, a clamor wells up from the remains. Rises and climbs higher. Causes convulsions in the bodies of the trunk-beings. Becomes an enormous groan between the gaps in the still-standing walls. Bores a pain in my head and my stomach. I try to reason with myself: a ghost can't suffer. He has neither a head nor a stomach. What's happening to me? Something has gone off kilter in me again and yet I'm dead. I wake with a start. Curled up, my hands between my thighs, I'd fallen asleep on the couch.

It's four in the morning. The rain has stopped. The wind is still gathering strength. Making the windowpanes bang. Nightmare or not, I really do have a headache and stomachache.

Aïcha was able to let Zana know I'm here. The woman is waiting for me at her home. Slim guides me toward the Montpellier suburb called "La Paillade."

The Grand Mail apartment building: a concrete slab imprisoned by concrete bars. Dismal. Deserted by the hordes of children who have transported their toys to other, kinder places. The stairwells remind me of Oran. Stench of garbage. Smashed letter-boxes. Broken-down elevators. Hallways made for horror films.

Zana's door. I knock. She opens. A shadow stares hard at me for a long time. I have difficulty distinguishing her features. In the apartment, darkness reigns. The woman comes toward me. Takes me in her arms and squeezes me endlessly. I let myself go in her embrace. Say to myself: what does her face matter, it is She. It is Zana. In my throat is a sob that refuses to come out.

She pulls open a curtain. The room fills with the day's grayness. I discover that I wouldn't have recognized Zana had I crossed her path in the street. Standing in the doorway, his skateboard on his shoulder, Slim tells me:

"I'll be back in a while."

Zana closes the door again.

"It's muggy! I don't like these winds from the south. They make me nervous. And then you suffocate."

"The sea is in a fury. Beautiful. It's invaded the whole beach."

"Have you been to the beach?"

"I'm staying in Palavas."

"Oh . . ."

She looks at me for a long time before dreamily adding:

"The first time I saw your mother, she talked to me about the sea. And it's the same with you. Fortunately, you don't have the same words to describe it. It's still a troubling coincidence."

"What did she say about the sea?"

"That it was almost her grave but Allah didn't want that."

"How do you mean, her grave?"

"Sometimes life goes even further than made-up stories and plunges us into a stupor."

Her elbows leaning on her knees, she joins her hands. Interlaces her fingers.

"You resemble her."

"Why was the sea almost her grave?"

"One day, I was on the train at the Marseilles station when a woman got on. Her eyes were wild and she had a bouquet of flowers in her hand. The car was still empty. She crossed it to come sit down facing me. Can you imagine that, a woman from home, with a square piece of cloth tied over two dresses, and some flowers as her only baggage? I was floored. When I tried to question her, she turned away toward the window and began to cry silently. She remained like that for the whole trip: a vacant look, beyond landscapes and time, her face streaming with tears. I let her cry in peace. I know how much good tears can do. Before the train came into the station here, I saw her preparing to get off. I said to her: 'I live in Montpellier. Do you want to come to my home?' She murmured: 'The ocean was almost my home, but Allah didn't want that.' I reiterated my invitation. She observed me through her tears for a long time and answered: 'Yes, thank you.' We spent more than a week together before she contacted her brother."

"But why was the ocean almost her grave?"

"Your father tore you from her arms. The next day she took the boat back to France. She said that she saw Oran grow more distant, then disappear behind a buoy. She said she felt as if she'd been cut in two. She said that she heard your cries and tears over the noise of the boat's machines. That the sea was calm. As calm as death. That she had a storm in her head. A black wind and screams of despair. That she didn't see herself reaching the other shore without you. She said she spent hours like that, torn apart, fascinated by the serenity of the blue waters. She said that all of a sudden she had the impression that the ocean was beginning to climb up, climb toward her and breathe her in."

"What do you mean?"

"What do I mean? When pain is intolerable, you have one desire: for it to stop. By whatever means. And death is a radical means by which everything stops. Definitively. Keltoum stepped over the guardrail and threw herself into the sea."

"But . . ."

"But she had incredible luck. Would you believe that on this boat there were a lot of French soldiers returning to France, since Algeria had just won its independence. Among them was an exceptional swimmer. From your mother's attitude, this man had guessed that she wasn't doing well. He wasn't far away when she weakened. Without waiting a second, the man dove in. He was able to catch her before she drowned. He held her head out of the water long enough for the boat to slow down and send a rowboat. If he hadn't been such a good swimmer, your mother would not have survived."

Shaking her head, Zana scrutinizes me. I'm too stunned, too downcast to respond.

"When she regained consciousness, Keltoum was at the Timone, a Marseilles hospital. It was night. She said that when she opened her eyes in the dark, she believed she was dead, lying on the bottom of the sea. She began to cry. A nurse came to comfort her and give her a sedative.

"The following morning the soldier who had saved her came

Of Dreams and Assassins

to visit. His eyes were the color of the sea, and he held a bouquet of flowers in his hand. In Arabic, he told her that life was beautiful, and that she was pretty. Nobody had ever before said that to her. She believed him.

"As soon as she was alone, she took her bundle and her flowers and ran away from the hospital. That's the morning we met each other.

"In spite of her sufferings, Keltoum loved life. And when she returned from the market, her basket was always decorated with a bouquet of flowers."

Slim took the bus to return home and go to the high school. We agreed to meet each other at around seven-thirty in the evening at the Place de la Comédie. I want to go to the meeting about Algeria. I spend the day with Zana.

I find Slim at a table in Les Trois Grâces café:

"Things okay?"

"Yes."

"Was what you learned good?"

"Well, no. But it did me good."

"How exactly?"

"Now my mother truly exists. I believe that I'm starting to love her. And that's priceless."

"What good does that do since she's dead?"

"It's especially because she's dead that it's good for something."

"And if you'd been told that she was a bitch or a don't-give-a-damn type, huh, what would you have done?"

"I have no idea."

"It's too easy to say: I have no idea. Everything fell in your lap, just like that, without you having to get off your ass! And there you are with your dilated eyes like a junkie who just had a fix, shit!"

"If she'd been an ignoble woman, not much would have

been said. And without a doubt that silence would have enlightened me. I would have left without further ado. To save myself."

"Without further ado, you believe that, do you! Your further ado, they'd have made you eat it, by will or by force. And the dirtier and stinkier, the more people enjoy themselves."

"You're pretty dark, all of a sudden."

"It must be my skin discoloring. Your stories and the ocean breeze get on my nerves."

"Listen, Slim, I'm crazy."

"Okay, okay, be egotistical. Now that you know everything, you want everyone to get off your back."

I shrug my shoulders. He calms down and starts staring at the crowd. The waiter arrives. I order a beer. We remain silent for a long time. Suddenly, Slim bursts out laughing. A joyful laugh with no bitterness. I'm delighted.

"What's happening to you?"

"You should have seen my street a little while ago! For real, Figuerolles is a village à la Clochemerle!"

"What happened?"

"A guy named Ali sold his business to a certain Brahim. Imagine Brahim arriving in the afternoon, proud as a bar-tobacco shop, accompanied by a painter. 'What's written up there?' He was pointing at the store's sign. 'Alimentation,' answered the painter. 'Okay, erase that for me and put 'Brahimentation!' Well, the poor painter had a difficult time making Brahim understand that alimentation had nothing to do with Ali. The whole street tried to help him see that. And they were gossiping! And they were cracking up!"

"How did it end?"

"A touching up of 'Alimentation,' and beside it, he had added 'Chez Brahim.'"

The room is packed. University faculty, lawyers, journalists . . . Analyses of thirty years of the FLN in power. Varied and contradictory criticism. Confused words, or those said in bad

Of Dreams and Assassins

faith by a few government apparatchiks, who are also there. Invectives from representatives of the assassins' sect. In the minority but equally present. Intertwining testimonies, which tell of the fear down there. The helplessness here. France, refusing them the status of refugees. The wounds that they would like to silence make their voices crack. The women stick to reality. Find the most pertinent, the most virulent words to denounce their exclusion and the martyrdom of women down there. Their courage impresses everyone. Slim leans toward me:

"The Algerian women are short but strong. They're intense . . . And say, do the democrats in Algeria always bicker like that?"

"They transport their quarrels to French territory because they're hunted down in Algeria. You know, a witticism from home says: 'They got along in order to never agree.' It was inspired by the dissensions at the heart of this fraud called the Arab world. The worst thing is that it turns out to be true inside the camps and clans in a given country."

A murmur goes across the room when a woman lawyer, who has been practicing in Montpellier for a long time, takes the floor.

"What's happening?" Slim asks his neighbor with concern.

"It seems she received telephone death threats this week."

"Is that possible? I'm dreaming! They're not going to do that to us here!"

"Do you see your Clochemerle turning into Bab El Oued?"

"No! She's known in the city. Some asshole or jealous fool just wanted to scare her out of her wits."

"It always starts like that: with assholes who want to spread fear."

At the end of the meeting, Roger Faure, Slim, and I go toward the woman. I ask her:

"Is it true you received death threats?"

"Who told you that?"

"It seems that it's not a secret from anyone."

She looks overwhelmed:

"People can't keep quiet!"

Of Dreams and Assassins

"Just what kind of threat was it?"

She hesitates a moment. Shrugs her shoulders. Her features become strained:

"Oh, since everybody knows: 'You're going to die, filthy dog! You're going to die, filthy dog!'"

"That's a threat from home."

"Yes. And it was a very young voice . . . Undoubtedly a Beur."

"Have you lodged a complaint?"

She turns toward Roger Faure, who seems very worried.

"Of course!"

Slim approaches her. Takes on a reassuring tone of voice: "Some asshole, for sure!"

The woman looks at him with a doubtful pout:

"I wish I could be sure of that."

I didn't want to have a drink with the participants. Didn't want to relive Algeria here. The words about my mother and those of the meeting clash in my head. Twist my innards. Back in Palavas, I run to the toilet and throw up.

I look at the sea. A while ago still, I felt no anxiety about the northern shore. No worry about this entity called the Mediterranean. Am I also going to become, whether I like it or not, a child of the northern shore? During this meeting a while ago, there weren't only Algerians. Far from it. Maghrebian Jews, *pieds-noirs*, French by birth or by blood . . . so many people felt concerned. Offered various services and to house the exiled. A sharing of efforts. I was overwhelmed. We were suddenly so close. I began to observe them. To become aware of other feelings of helplessness. Other loves mutilated or fallen into bitterness when forgetting is impossible. How many of us have had our memories torn apart? Our frustrations expressed or silenced? Our loves made painful or nostalgic? Our gaze constantly turned toward the other shore? We are affection woven between the South and the North.

Of Dreams and Assassins

Cultures, memories crossbred by the North and the South. And the waves caressing Tunis, Algiers, Oran, or Tangiers give us shivers even beyond Marseilles, Montpellier, and Perpignan.

I look at the sea. Will it ever manage to heal me of Algerian traumatisms? Of my rage?

I look at the sea. Think of my mother. Of the desert and of Alilou. I listen to the wind. I can't eat or sleep. Can't move. My stomach is burning. And further down I have cramps. The wind is wailing about the South's pain. It churns the sea. Carries me away toward other white lands. Far from everything. All this to-do about my origins, this sea spray of freedom.

At five o'clock in the morning, my decision is made. I close up my suitcase. Make myself some coffee. Call a taxi for the Montpellier train station. Men sweeping. A few tramps are still asleep. I buy my ticket and a newspaper. Wait for seven o'clock to telephone Slim's house.

"Slim is still sleeping."

"Don't wake him. I wanted to say a big thanks to you. I'm leaving."

"Where? For Algeria? Already!"

"No, no. I'm going to see a friend in Paris. Then I'll go to Canada. Tell Slim I'll write to him."

"Are you going to stay there?"

"No, I want to travel. Good-bye, Khadidja, I'm taking the seven-fifty TGV."

I'm on the train when Slim flashes onto the platform on his roller blades. Bumps into people. Comes toward my window:

"What's gotten into you? What happened?"

"I want to travel. Travel to countries where I have no roots. Like you."

"Will you come back?"

"Yes."

"For sure, you're not fibbing?"

"I promise you, and we'll be able to talk."

"When?"

"I don't know."

The train sets off. I motion to him with my hand. At the moment I'm leaving Montpellier, the face of the woman lawyer I saw yesterday haunts my thoughts. And in the rolling sound of the train I hear: "You're going to die, filthy dog! You're going to die, filthy dog! You're going to die, filthy dog!"

"Hey, madame, I don't know!"

Slim glides along the platform and accompanies the train.

"Send me a bunch of postcards."

"I promise."

I see so many questions in his eyes. My heart feels a pang of anguish.

"You're too much!"

He bursts out laughing. And in a wild pirouette blows me a kiss before disappearing behind a column. That image of his radiant laughter is what I want to keep from Montpellier.

Montpellier flies by my window. Roger Faure had invited me for dinner this evening. I'll have to remember to telephone him from Paris to cancel.

Glossary

Aïcha: The living one, the one carried by life.

Algé-Riens: A play on words. An Algérois is an inhabitant of Algiers. *Rois* means "kings," and *Algé-Rois* means the "Kings of Algiers." *Rien* means "nothing." *Algérien* means "Algerian." So the pun *Algé-Riens* means "the Algerians with nothing." The "Kings of Algiers," i.e., the privileged classes, are being compared to the more impoverished, the "Algerians with nothing."

Ali Bel Hadj: A leader of the FIS.

Bab El Oued: A neighborhood of Algiers, a hotbed of unrest, Islamic fundamentalism, and violence.

baraka: Good luck.

barka: Enough.

bearded ones: The Islamists who traditionally wear beards.

Beur: The first-generation descendants of North African immigrants to France, especially Algerian. A body of Beur literature has developed in the 1980s and 1990s. The word itself is a play on the spelling of the word *Arabe.* A pun is made with the word *beurre,* which means butter but sounds like *beur.*

Blek le Roc: French robot cartoon character.

bojor: Bonjour, hello.

Boudiaf, Mohammed: An Algerian president assassinated in the early 1990s. One of the main founders and leaders of the FLN.

Brassens, Georges: A popular French singer.

Chadli, Benjedid: A colonel who was designated president of Algeria in 1979; he remained in office until 1992, when he was forced by the army to step down, for fear that he wanted to cooperate with the Islamic fundamentalists.

chador: A veil and long cloak intended to completely hide a woman's body in public.

Clochemerle: The title of a 1934 comic novel by Gabriel Chevalier about the scandal caused in a fictitious small Beaujolais town when a public urinal was installed next to the church. This is an allusion to the novel and the scandal caused among the pious by such a practical (male) public convenience.

Comité de Défense des Intellectuels Algériens: Committee for the Defense of Algerian Intellectuals.

Djeha: A malicious character from Algerian legend.

douar: A rural administrative division.

entchadorées: Women wearing the chador, a black cloth covering for the head, most of the face, and the body, which is put on over the clothes.

fatwa: A religious edict in the Muslim religion; can include a call for assassination of those considered to be offending the religion.

FIS: Le Front Islamique du Salut (the Islamic Salvation Front), one of the main fundamentalist Islamic groups.

Fissistes: Those who belong to the FIS.

FLN: Front de Libération Nationale (the National Liberation Front), the sole state-run party, until uprisings in 1988 forced the government to allow a plurality of political parties.

francis: French

ghurba: Exile.

Goldorac: Futuristic French robot cartoon character.

hamada: A rocky plateau found in desert regions.

hidjab: A form of women's covering; often black, very long, going all the way to the ankles, covering the head with a triangular headdress.

hittistes: Literally, "those who hold up the walls." The unemployed, loiterers.

inshallah: God willing.

Glossary

Kalachnikov: A high-powered Russian machine gun.

khalti: Aunt, a term marking respect.

khbayti: Drunkard.

khoroto: Whatever *métèque,* a pejorative for a dark-skinned person.

laïco-assimilationnistes: An expression used by the FLN to refer to those whom they accuse of wanting to continue close association with France and therefore to be secular and more French than Algerian.

L'aid: Aïd al fitr is the feast celebrating the breaking of the Ramadan fast. Aïd al ad'ha is the feast of sacrifice.

maître-assistant: A tenure-track rank in the French university system.

makayensh: There isn't any; nothing.

malayque: A kind of surface algae that makes ponds smell bad. "Pue-la-vase," meaning "stinky sludge" or "mud," is a pun on the name of the area next to Montpellier named Palavas-les-Flots.

medersa: A Koranic school.

menshar: A saw, symbol of satire, indeed even of slander.

meskina: The poor thing.

"Mets de l'huile": "Put Oil On," a song by the Montpellier group Regg'lyss.

meyda: Low table.

mima: A nickname for mother.

Minitel: French national computer network, available for subscription through the post office.

ninjas: Masked elite troops belonging to the police and taking their name from the Ninja Turtles.

pied-noir: The French of Algeria.

qsar: A traditional village built of earth and hardened mud.

rahma: Mercy.

raï: One of the most popular forms of Algerian music, originating in eastern Algeria in the 1920s.

Ramadan: Fasting during the month of Ramadan is one of the obligations of Islam.

regg: Rocky desert geological form.

Glossary

RMI: Revenue Minimum d'Insertion; unemployment benefits paid after initial unemployment benefits have been exhausted. For people over twenty-five years old.

serwal: Wide-shaped pants worn in North Africa.

sha'abi, andalou: Types of music performed and listened to in Algeria.

shikaya: Complaints, quarreling.

smala: A large family.

SNED: Société Nationale d'Edition et de Diffusion. A state-run publishing house.

Sonacotra: A large company based in southern France.

Targou: A female ghost from Algerian legend.

Tartine: A French children's story character.

Tati: Name of a discount department-store chain where many North Africans shop.

TGV: "Train à Grande Vitesse"; high-speed train.

Tintin: Famous French comic-book character invented by Hergé in the 1950s.

tshitshis: The young jet set.

ya lalla: Oh, madame.

ya rebbi: Oh, my God.

zaa'ma: So-called.

zazou: Name given, during the Second World War, to young men who called attention to themselves because of their love for American jazz and their flashy elegance.

zufris: Workers.

CARAF Books
Caribbean and African Literature
Translated from French

A number of writers from very different cultures in Africa and the Caribbean continue to write in French although their daily communication may be in another language. While this use of French brings their creative vision to a more diverse international public, it inevitably enriches and often deforms the conventions of classical French, producing new regional idioms worthy of notice in their own right. The works of these francophone writers offer valuable insights into a highly varied group of complex and evolving cultures. The CARAF Books series was founded in an effort to make these works available to a public of English-speaking readers.

For students, scholars, and general readers, CARAF offers selected novels, short stories, plays, poetry, and essays that have attracted attention across national boundaries. In most cases the works are published in English for the first time. The specialists presenting the works have often interviewed the author in preparing background materials, and each title includes an original essay situating the work within its own literary and social context and offering a guide to thoughtful reading.

CARAF Books

Guillaume Oyônô-Mbia and Seydou Badian
Faces of African Independence:
Three Plays
Translated by Clive Wake

Olympe Bhêly-Quénum
Snares without End
Translated by Dorothy S. Blair

Bertène Juminer
The Bastards
Translated by Keith Q. Warner

Tchicaya U Tam'Si
The Madman and the Medusa
Translated by Sonja Haussmann Smith
and William Jay Smith

Alioum Fantouré
Tropical Circle
Translated by Dorothy S. Blair

Edouard Glissant
Caribbean Discourse: Selected Essays
Translated by J. Michael Dash

Daniel Maximin
Lone Sun
Translated by Nidra Poller

Aimé Césaire
Lyric and Dramatic Poetry, 1946–82
Translated by Clayton Eshleman
and Annette Smith

René Depestre
The Festival of the Greasy Pole
Translated by Carrol F. Coates

Kateb Yacine
Nedjma
Translated by Richard Howard

Léopold Sédar Senghor
The Collected Poetry
Translated by Melvin Dixon

Maryse Condé
I, Tituba, Black Witch of Salem
Translated by Richard Philcox

Assia Djebar
Women of Algiers in Their Apartment
Translated by Marjolijn de Jager

Dany Bébel-Gisler
Leonora: The Buried Story of Guadeloupe
Translated by Andrea Leskes

Lilas Desquiron
Reflections of Loko Miwa
Translated by Robin Orr Bodkin

Jacques Stephen Alexis
General Sun, My Brother
Translated by Carrol F. Coates

Malika Mokeddem
Of Dreams and Assassins
Translated by K. Melissa Marcus